W9-BNE-353

Masters of Spinjitzu

#3 RISE OF THE SERPENTINE

Greg Farshtey • Writer

Paul Lee,
with Space Goat
and Paulo Henrique • Artists

Laurie E. Smith • Colorist

PAPERCUTZ
New York

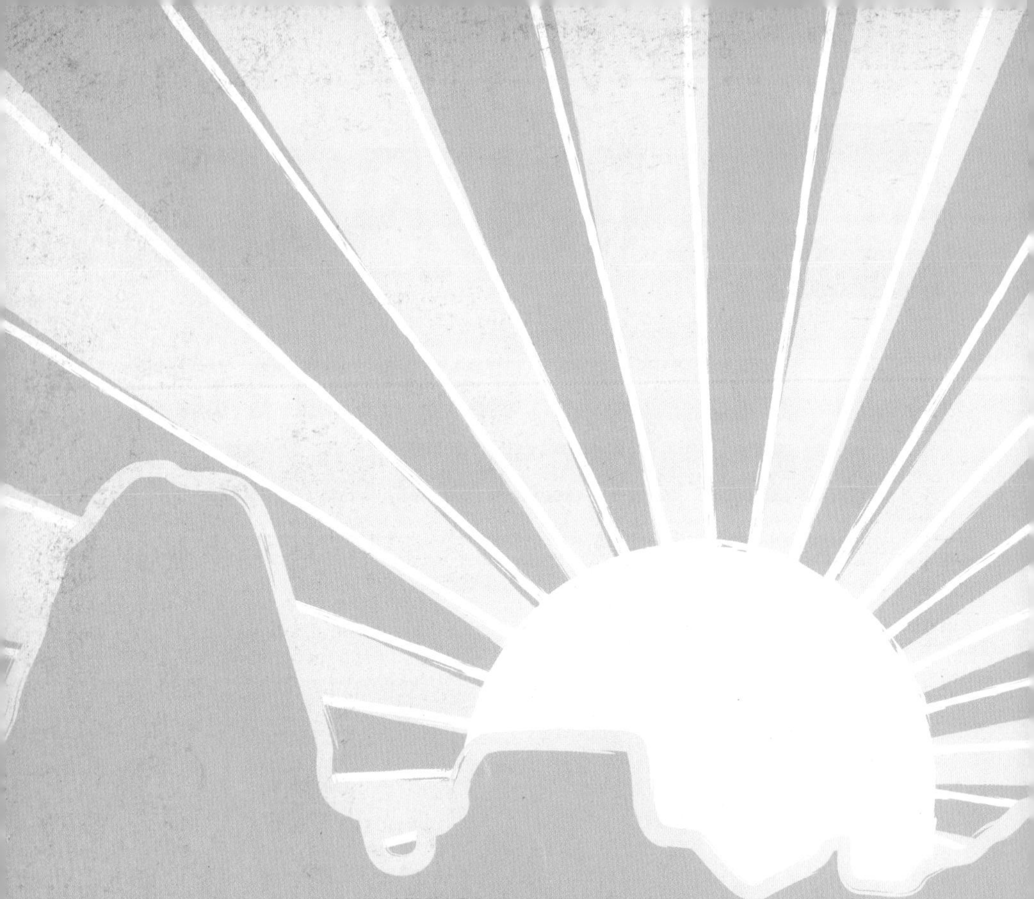

NINJAGO Masters of Spinjitzu
3 "Rise of the Serpentine"

GREG FARSHTEY – Writer
PAUL LEE
With SPACE GOAT and
PAULO HENRIQUE – Artists
LAURIE E. SMITH – Colorist
CHRIS CHUCKRY – Color Assist
BRYAN SENKA and TOM ORZECHOWSKI– Letterers

Production by NELSON DESIGN GROUP, LLC
Associate Editor – MICHAEL PETRANEK
JIM SALICRUP
Editor-in-Chief

ISBN: 978-1-59707-325-7 paperback edition
ISBN: 978-1-59707-326-4 hardcover edition

Printed in US
August 2012 by Lifetouch Printing
5126 Forest Hills Ct
Loves Park, IL 61111

Distributed by Macmillan

Second Printing

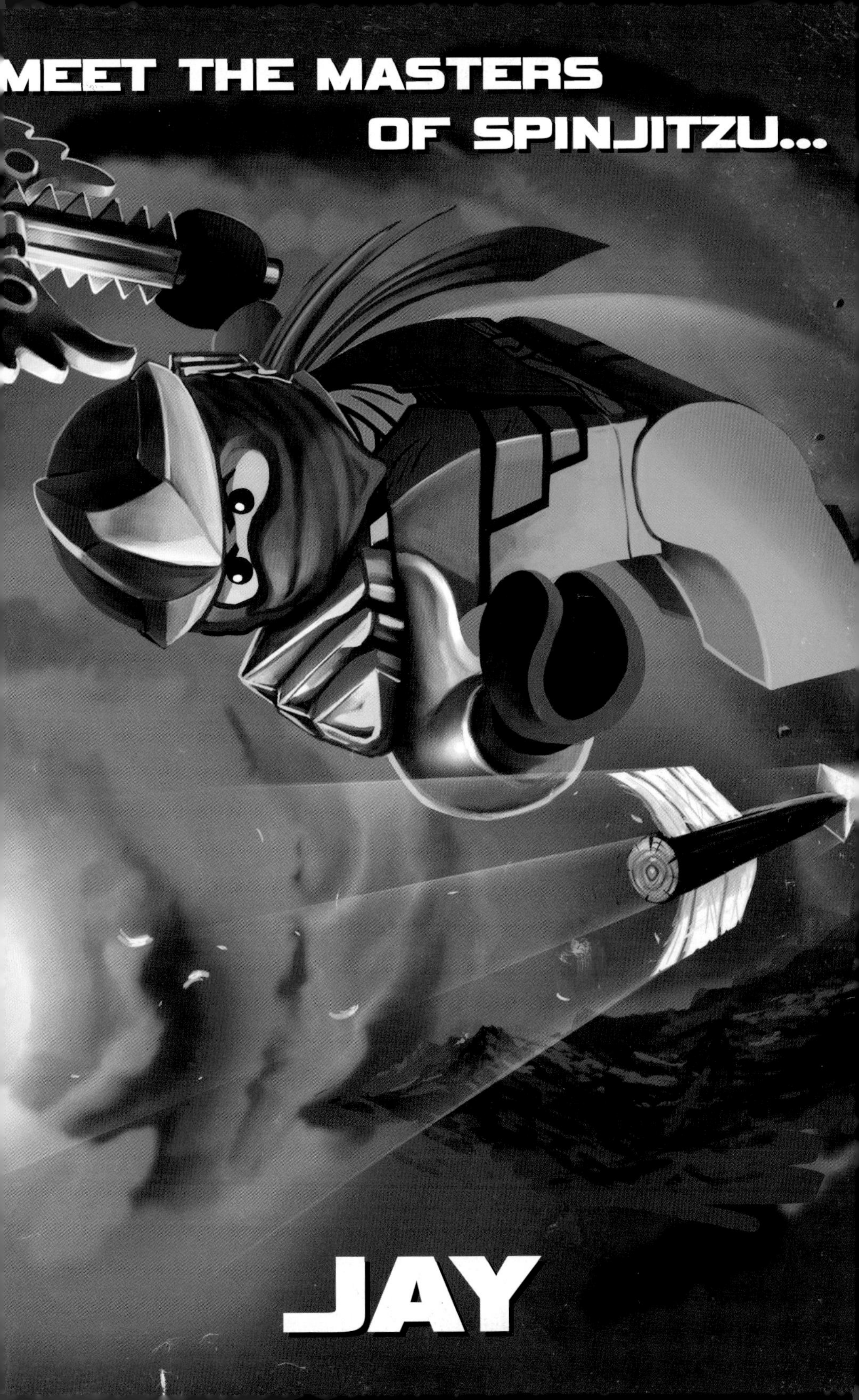
MEET THE MASTERS
OF SPINJITZU...
JAY

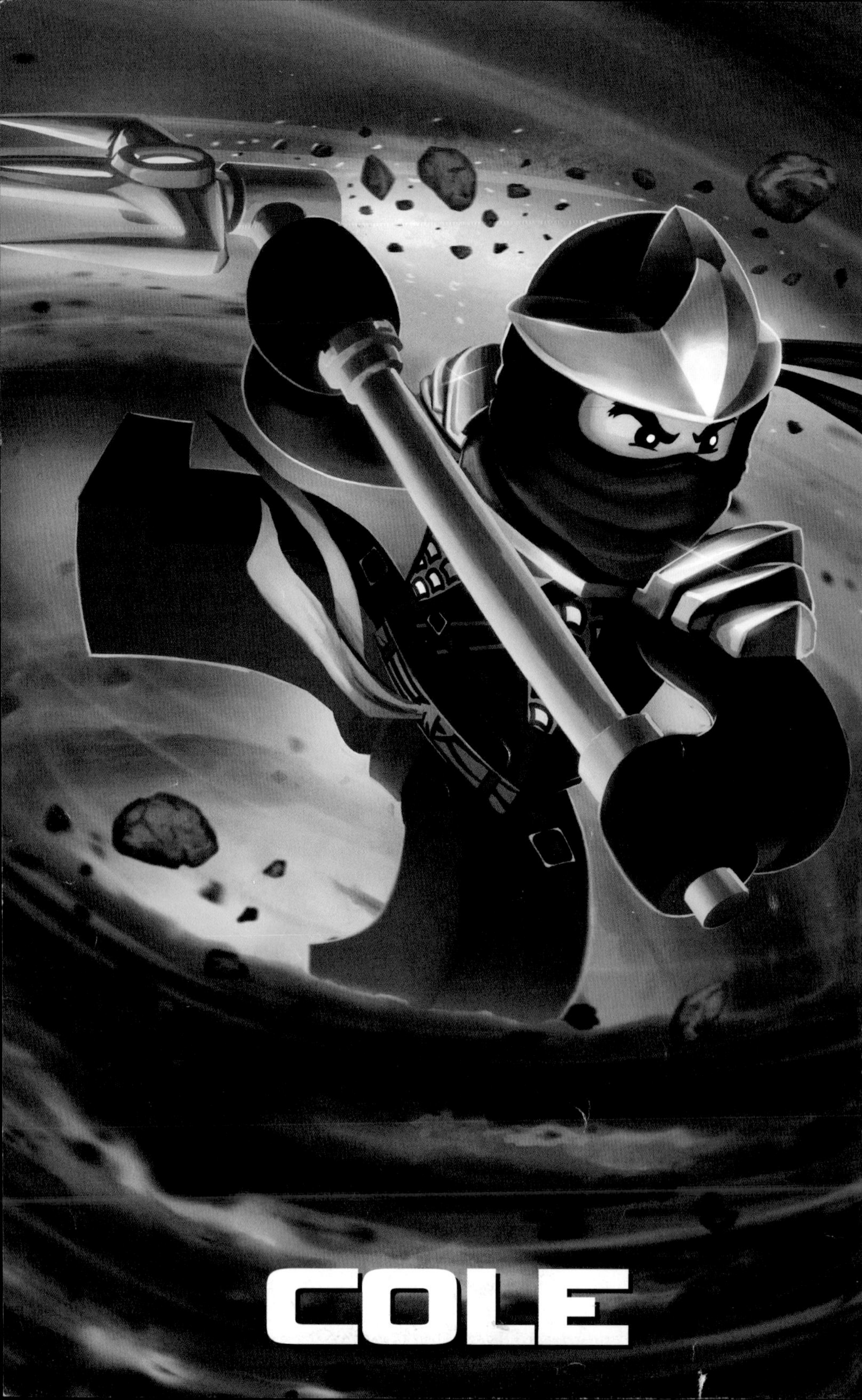
COLE

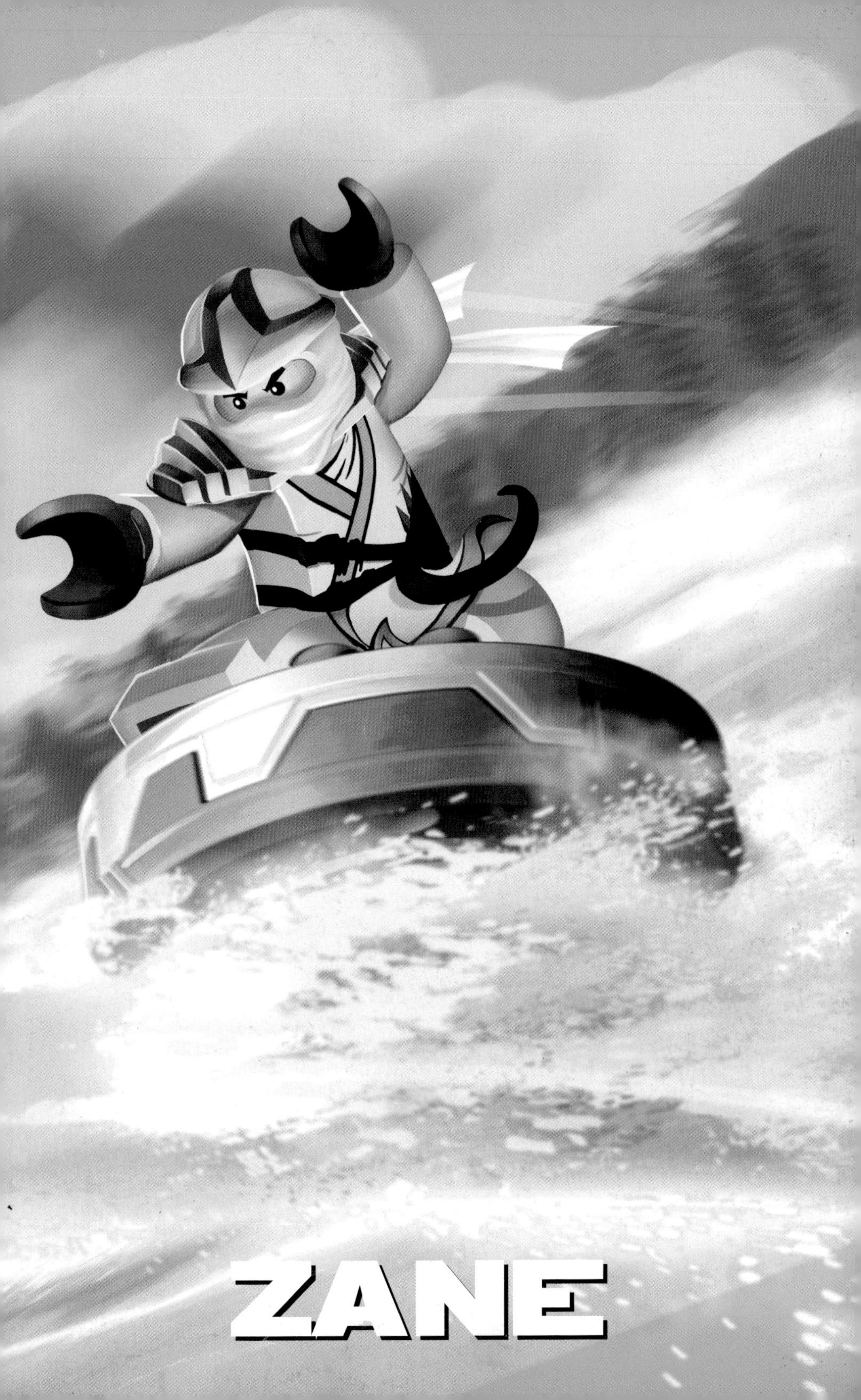
ZANE

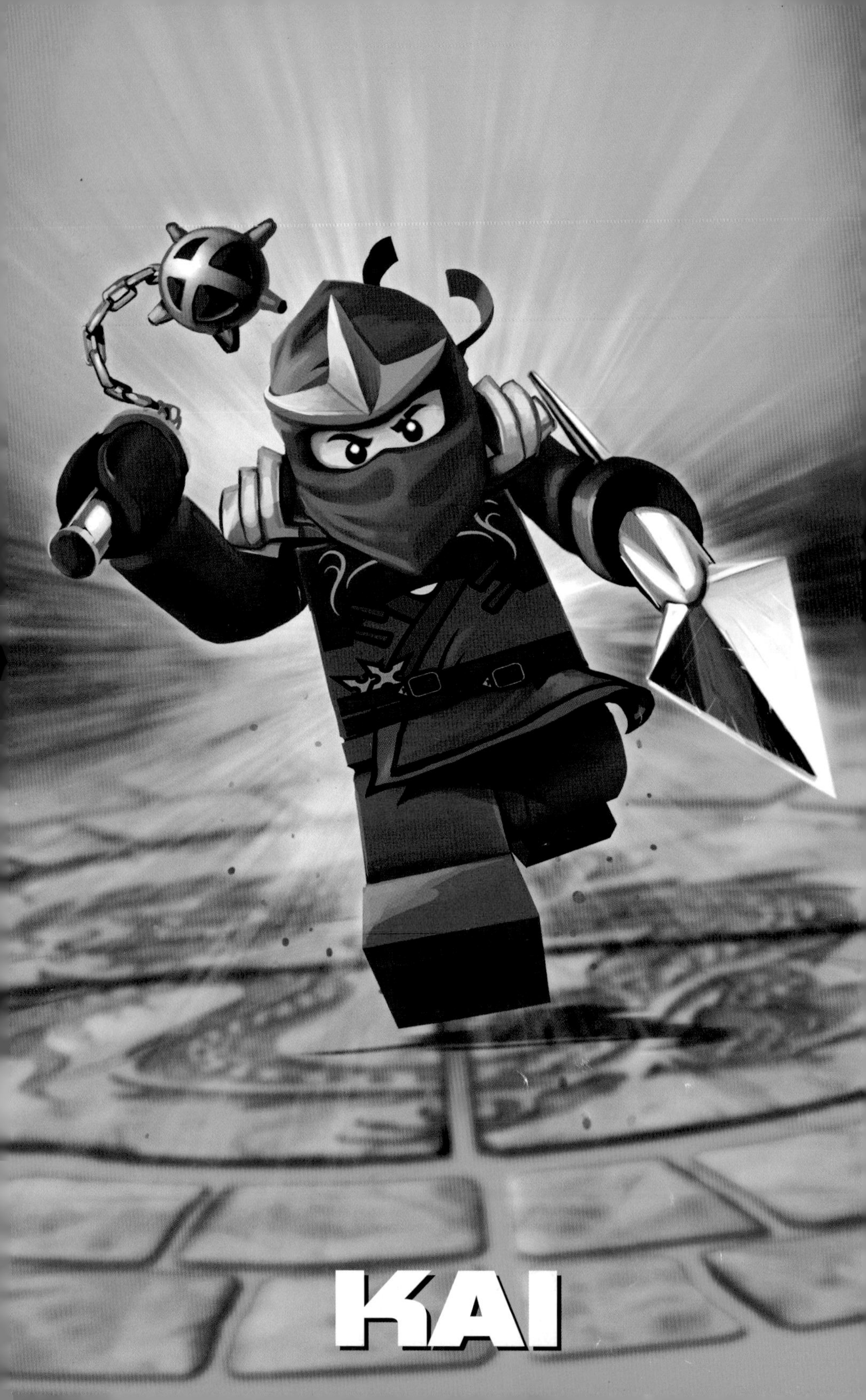
KAI

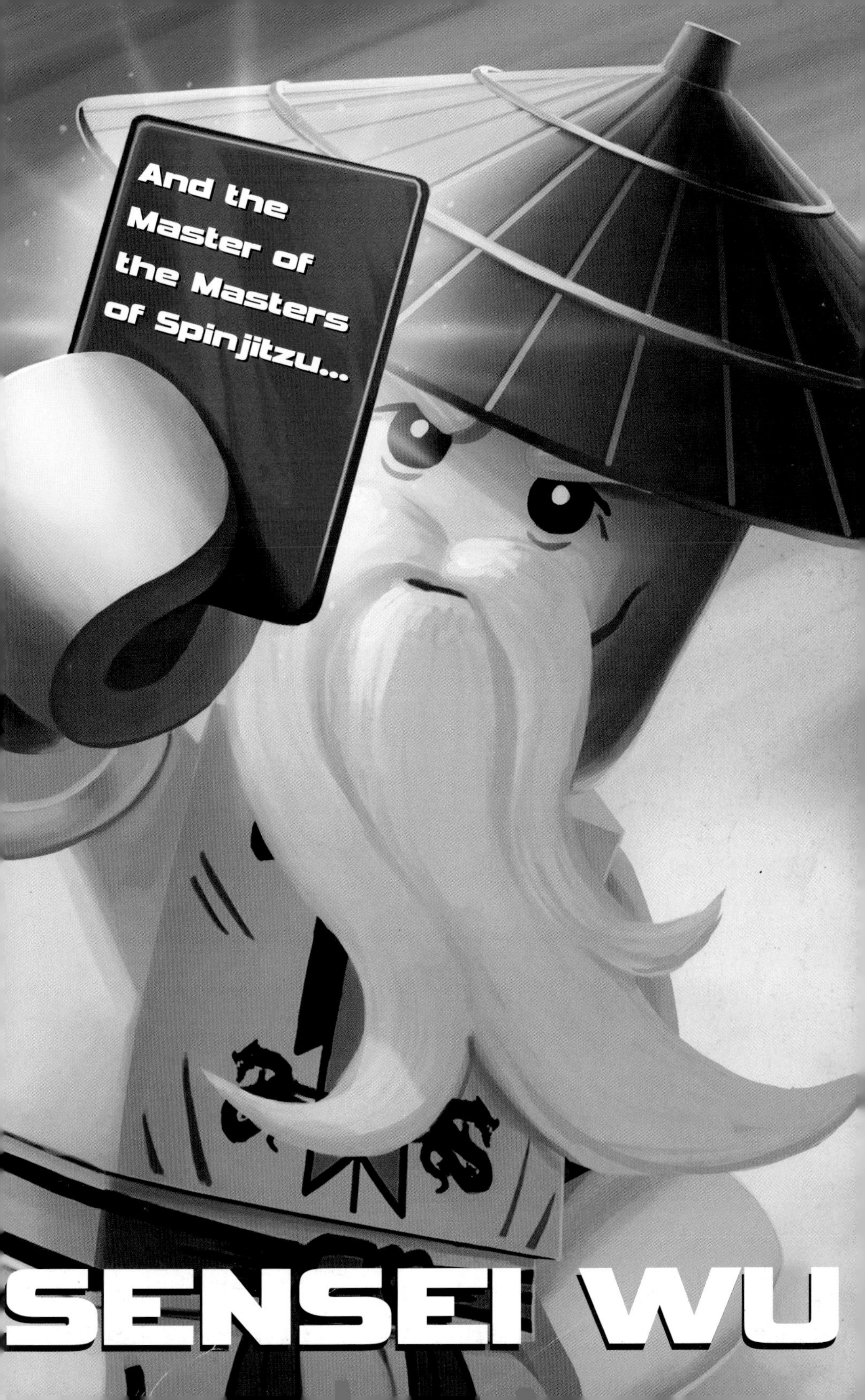
And the Master of the Masters of Spinjitzu...
SENSEI WU

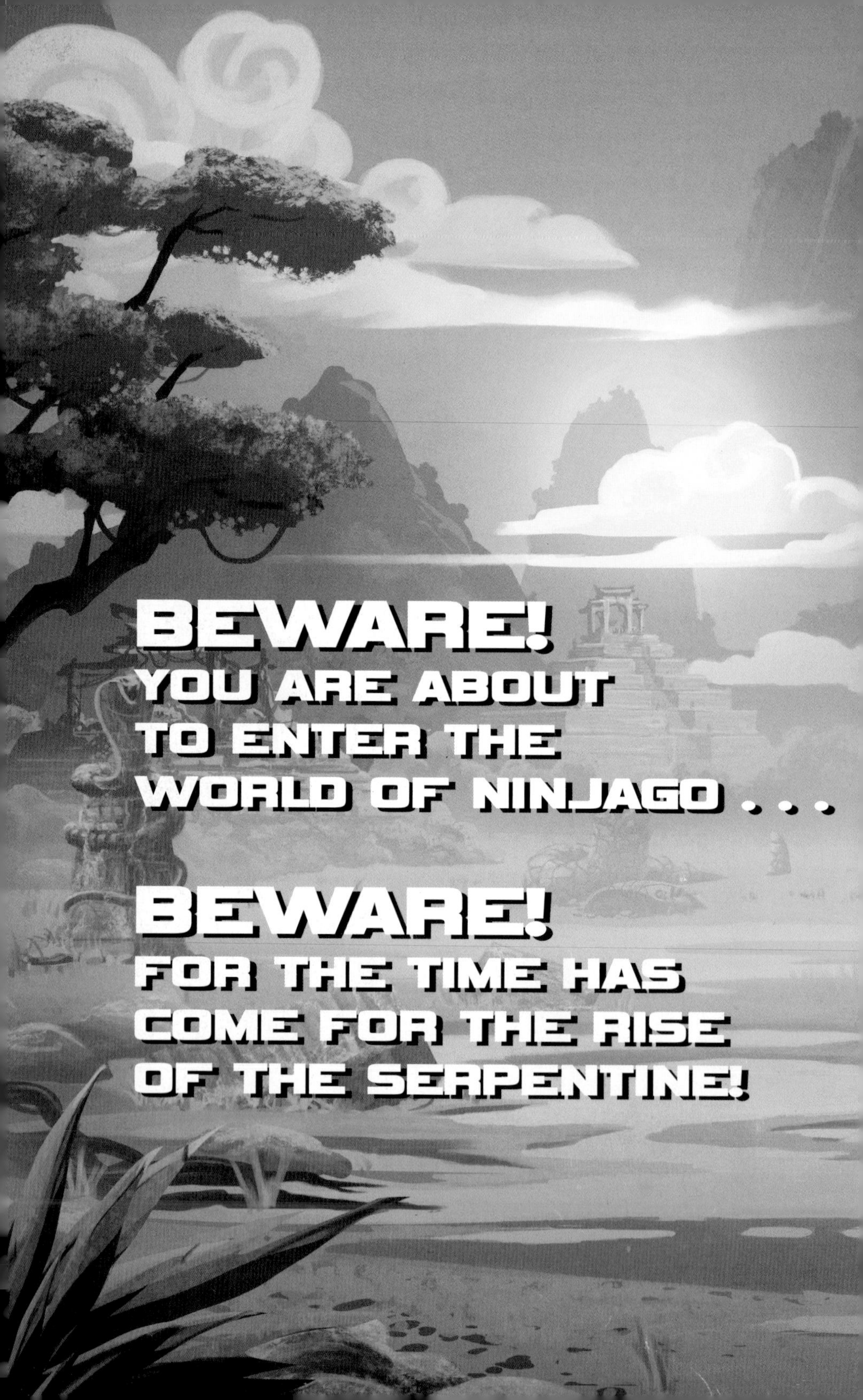
BEWARE!
YOU ARE ABOUT
TO ENTER THE
WORLD OF NINJAGO . . .
BEWARE!
FOR THE TIME HAS
COME FOR THE RISE
OF THE SERPENTINE!

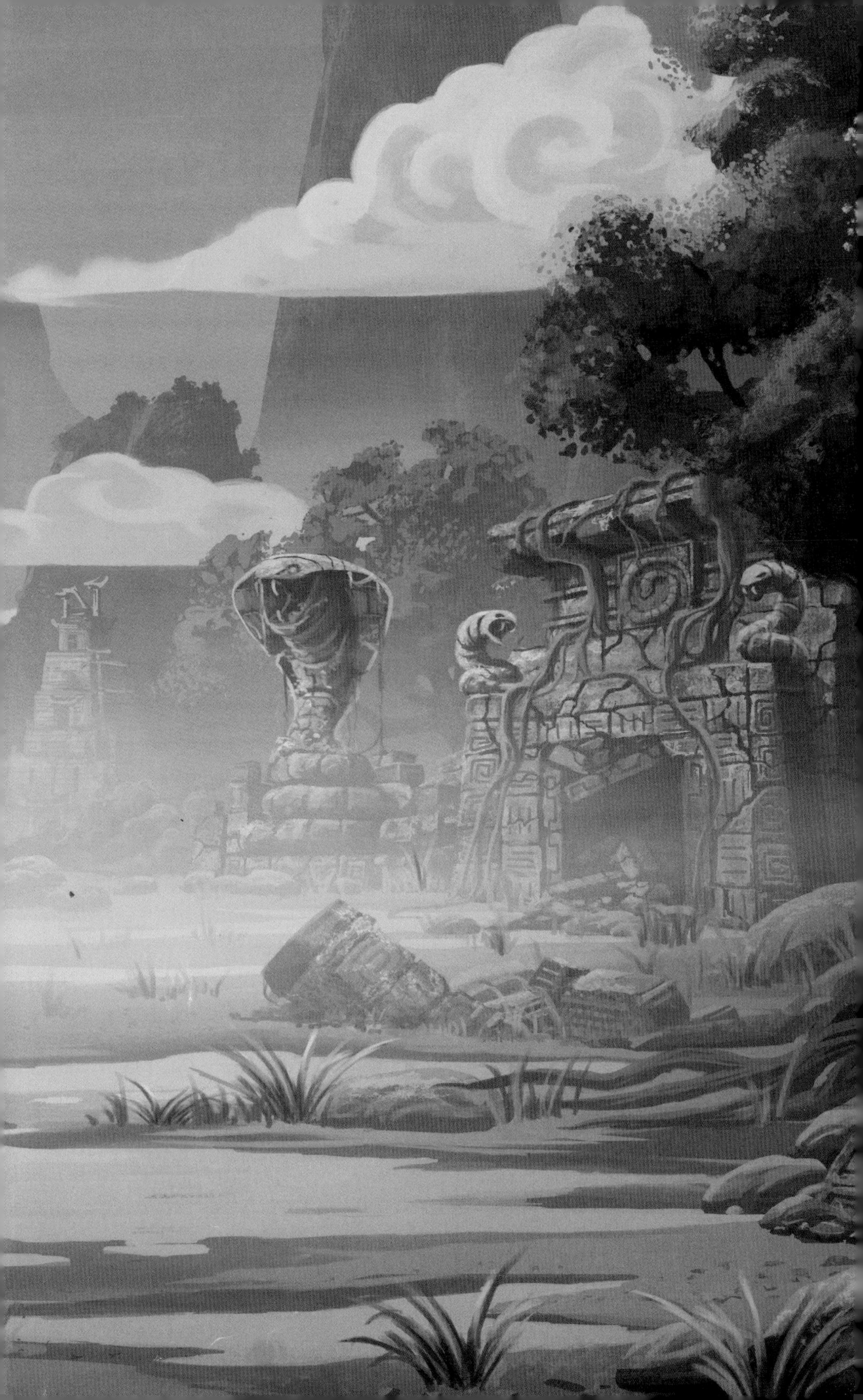

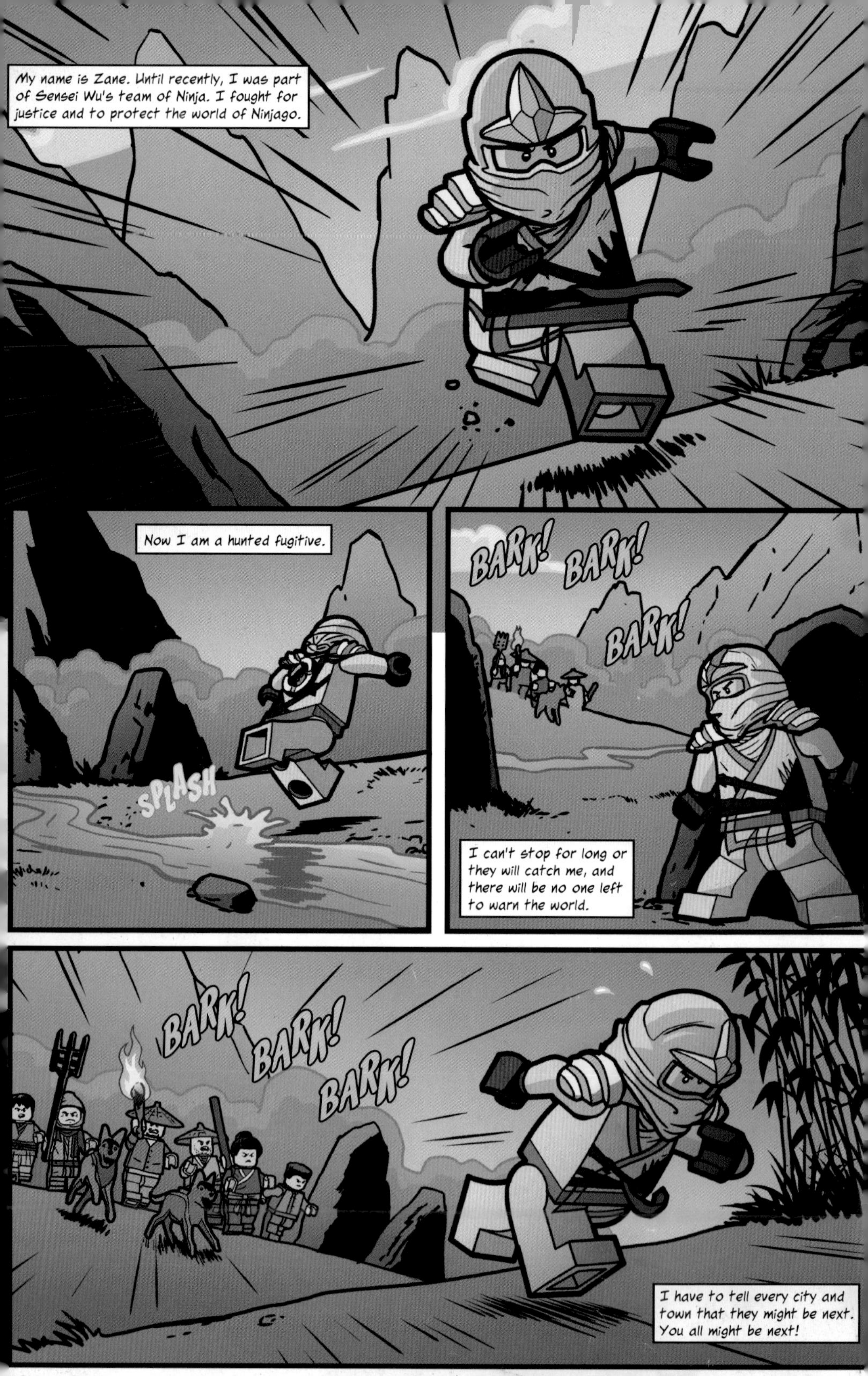
My name is Zane. Until recently, I was part of Sensei Wu's team of Ninja. I fought for justice and to protect the world of Ninjago.
Now I am a hunted fugitive.
SPLASH
BARK! BARK!
BARK!
I can't stop for long or they will catch me, and there will be no one left to warn the world.
BARK!
BARK!
BARK!
I have to tell every city and town that they might be next. You all might be next!

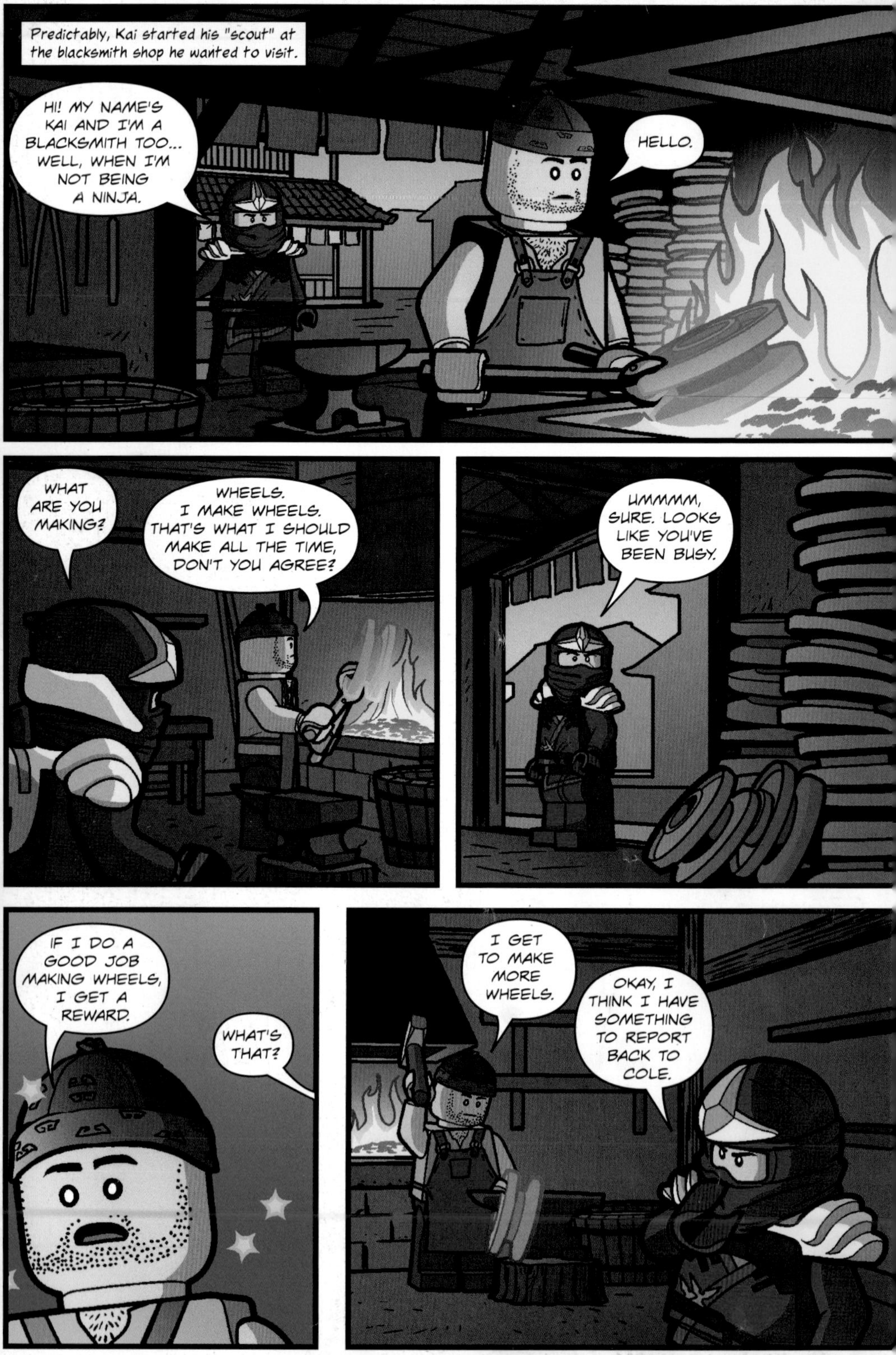
Predictably, Kai started his "scout" at the blacksmith shop he wanted to visit.
HI! MY NAME'S KAI AND I'M A BLACKSMITH TOO... WELL, WHEN I'M NOT BEING A NINJA.
HELLO.
WHAT ARE YOU MAKING?
WHEELS. I MAKE WHEELS. THAT'S WHAT I SHOULD MAKE ALL THE TIME, DON'T YOU AGREE?
UMMMMM, SURE. LOOKS LIKE YOU'VE BEEN BUSY.
IF I DO A GOOD JOB MAKING WHEELS, I GET A REWARD.
WHAT'S THAT?
I GET TO MAKE MORE WHEELS.
OKAY, I THINK I HAVE SOMETHING TO REPORT BACK TO COLE.

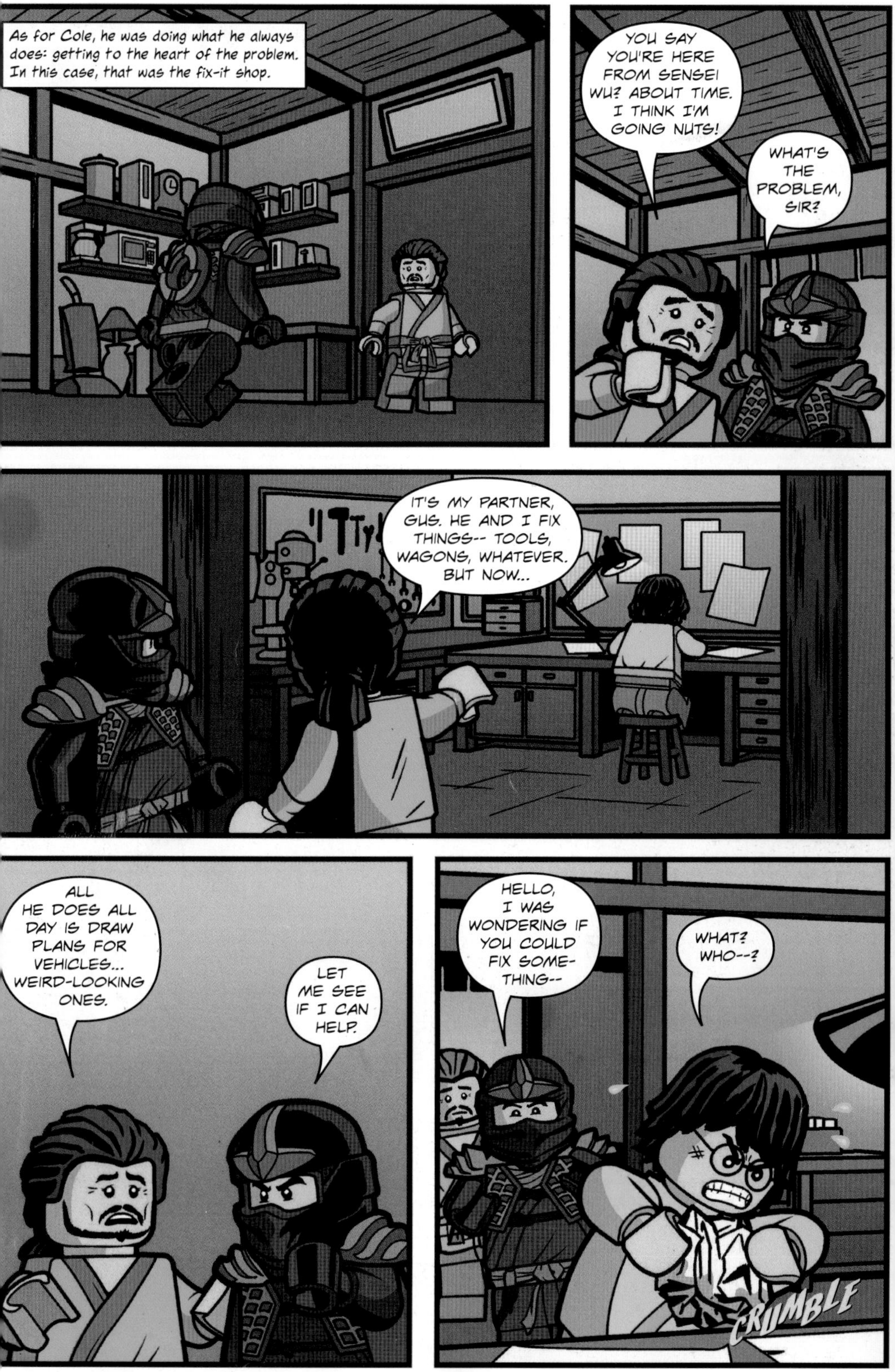
As for Cole, he was doing what he always does: getting to the heart of the problem. In this case, that was the fix-it shop.
YOU SAY YOU'RE HERE FROM SENSEI WU? ABOUT TIME. I THINK I'M GOING NUTS!
WHAT'S THE PROBLEM, SIR?
IT'S MY PARTNER, GUS. HE AND I FIX THINGS-- TOOLS, WAGONS, WHATEVER. BUT NOW...
ALL HE DOES ALL DAY IS DRAW PLANS FOR VEHICLES... WEIRD-LOOKING ONES.
LET ME SEE IF I CAN HELP.
HELLO, I WAS WONDERING IF YOU COULD FIX SOME-THING--
WHAT? WHO--?
CRUMBLE

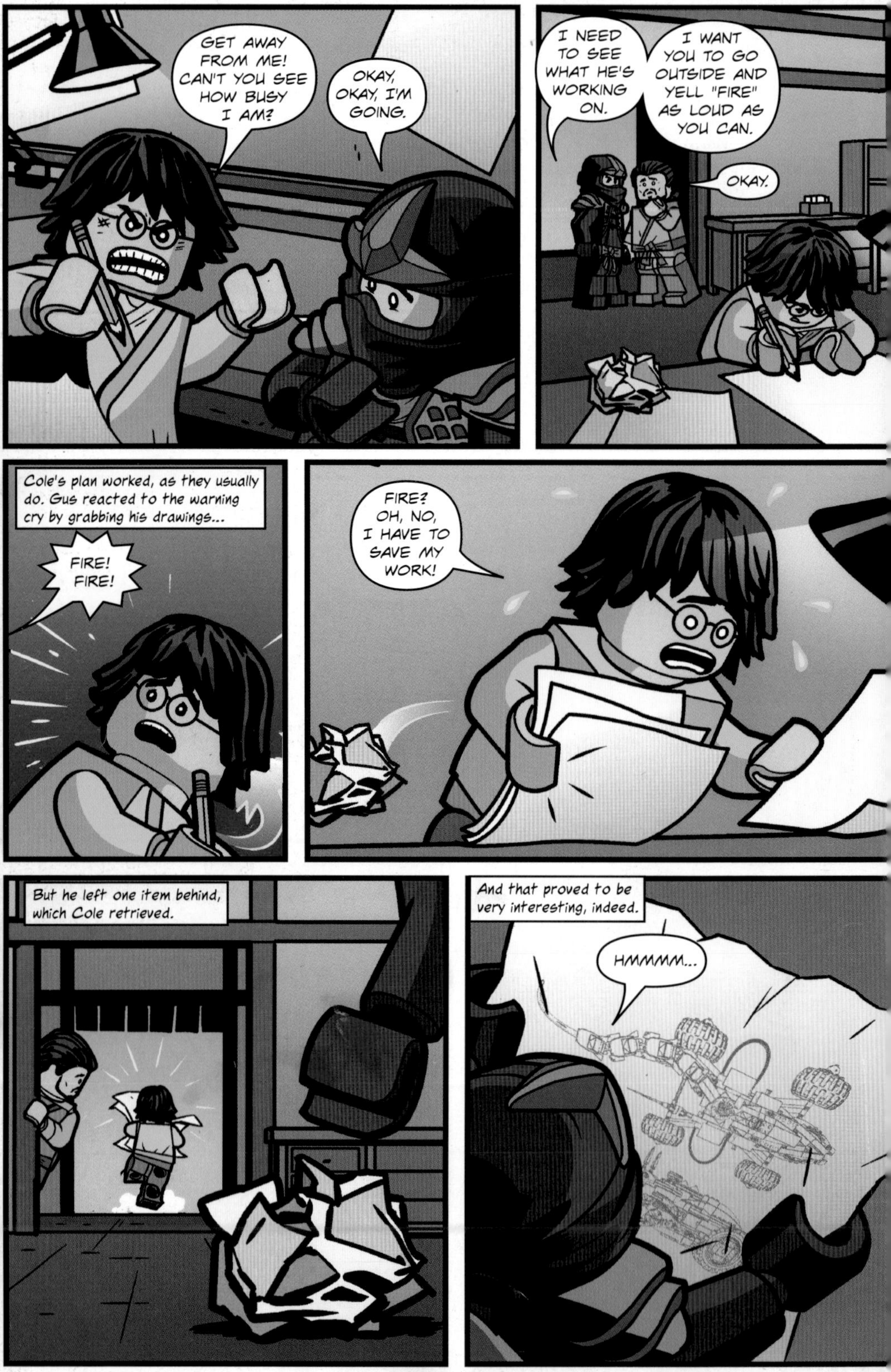
GET AWAY FROM ME! CAN'T YOU SEE HOW BUSY I AM?
OKAY, OKAY, I'M GOING.
I NEED TO SEE WHAT HE'S WORKING ON.
I WANT YOU TO GO OUTSIDE AND YELL "FIRE" AS LOUD AS YOU CAN.
OKAY.
Cole's plan worked, as they usually do. Gus reacted to the warning cry by grabbing his drawings...
FIRE! FIRE!
FIRE? OH, NO, I HAVE TO SAVE MY WORK!
But he left one item behind, which Cole retrieved.
And that proved to be very interesting, indeed.
HMMMM...

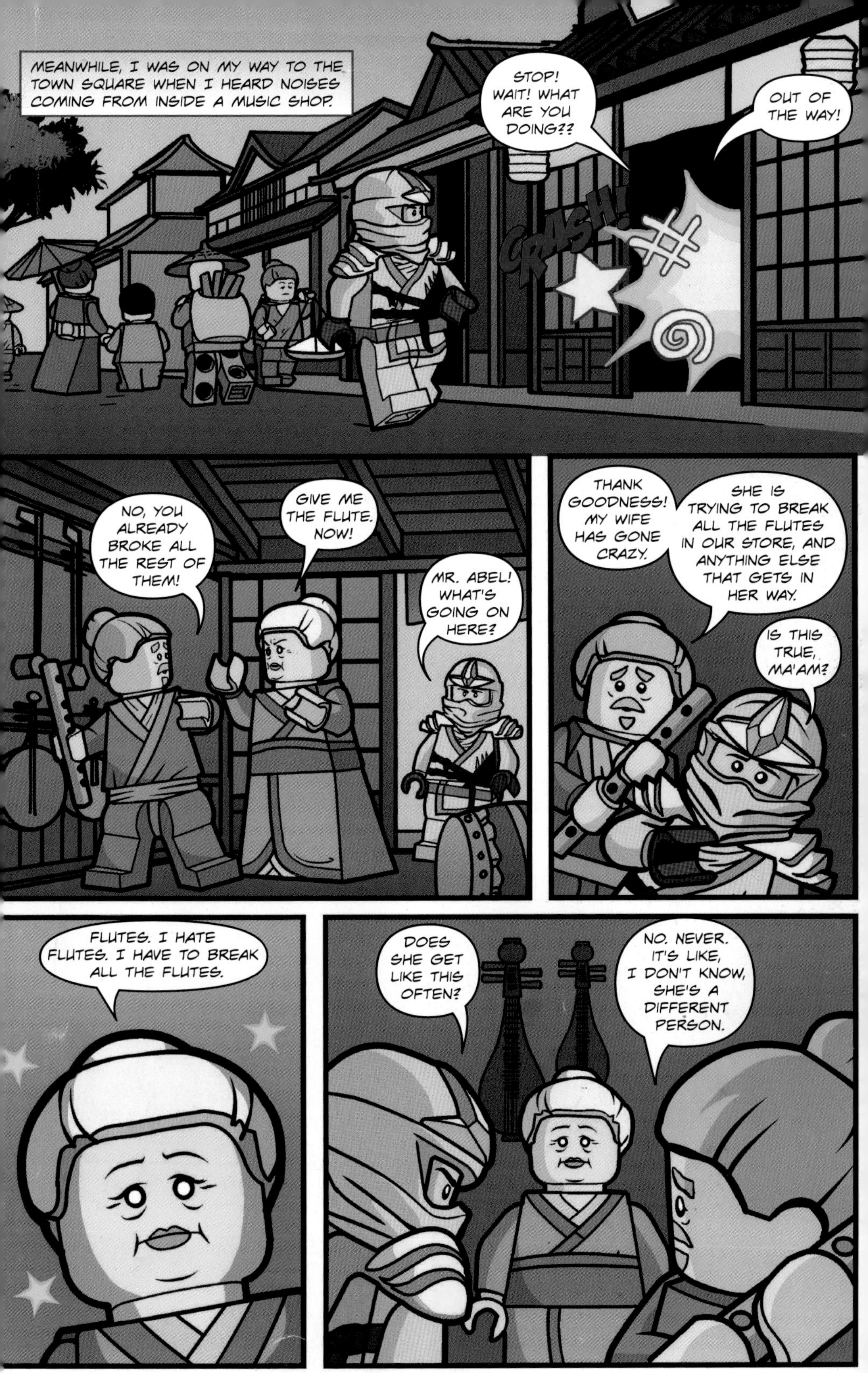
MEANWHILE, I WAS ON MY WAY TO THE TOWN SQUARE WHEN I HEARD NOISES COMING FROM INSIDE A MUSIC SHOP.
STOP! WAIT! WHAT ARE YOU DOING??
OUT OF THE WAY!
CRASH!
NO, YOU ALREADY BROKE ALL THE REST OF THEM!
GIVE ME THE FLUTE. NOW!
MR. ABEL! WHAT'S GOING ON HERE?
THANK GOODNESS! MY WIFE HAS GONE CRAZY.
SHE IS TRYING TO BREAK ALL THE FLUTES IN OUR STORE, AND ANYTHING ELSE THAT GETS IN HER WAY.
IS THIS TRUE, MA'AM?
FLUTES. I HATE FLUTES. I HAVE TO BREAK ALL THE FLUTES.
DOES SHE GET LIKE THIS OFTEN?
NO. NEVER. IT'S LIKE, I DON'T KNOW, SHE'S A DIFFERENT PERSON.

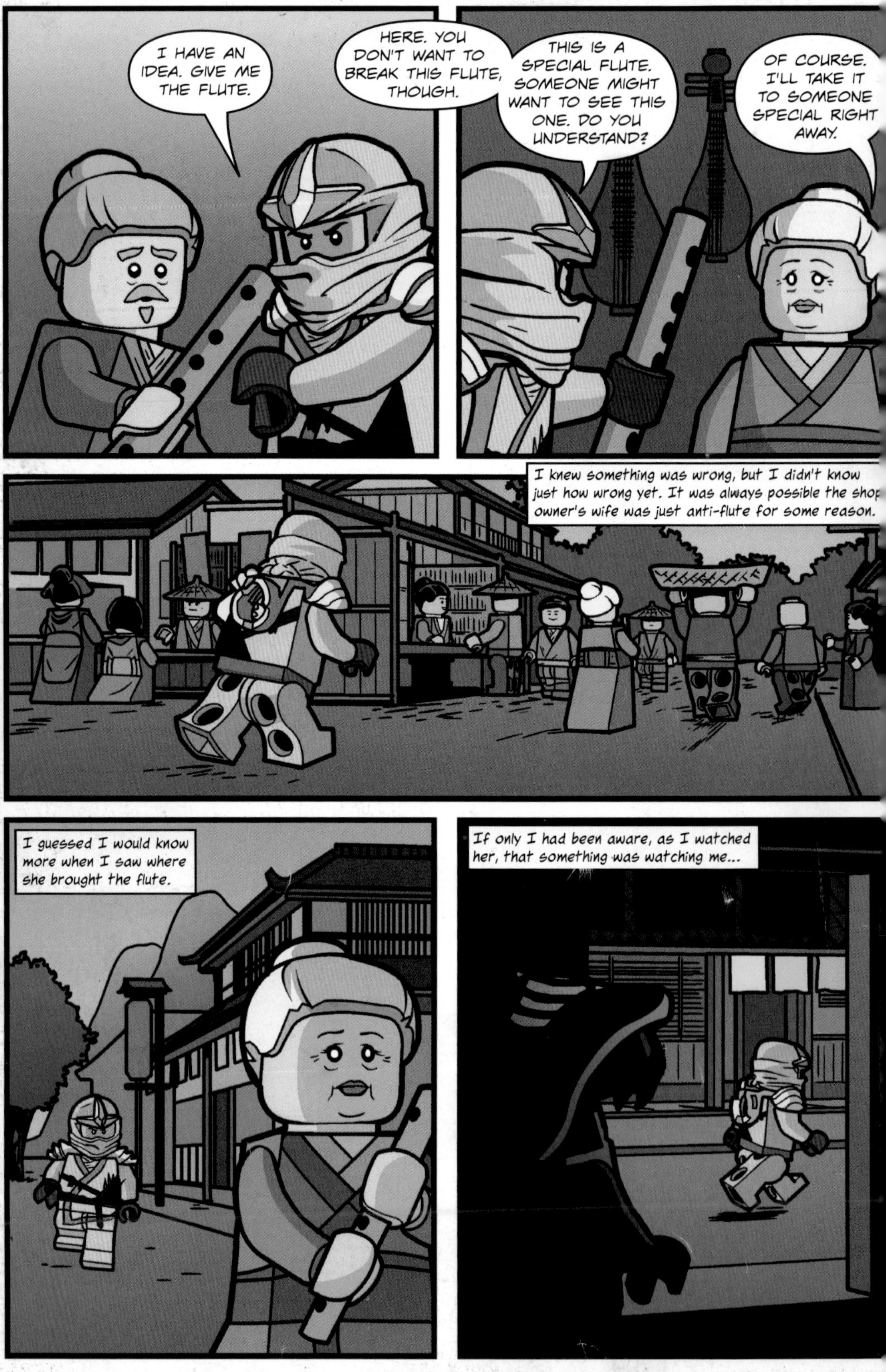

I HAVE AN IDEA. GIVE ME THE FLUTE.
HERE. YOU DON'T WANT TO BREAK THIS FLUTE, THOUGH.
THIS IS A SPECIAL FLUTE. SOMEONE MIGHT WANT TO SEE THIS ONE. DO YOU UNDERSTAND?
OF COURSE. I'LL TAKE IT TO SOMEONE SPECIAL RIGHT AWAY.
I knew something was wrong, but I didn't know just how wrong yet. It was always possible the shop owner's wife was just anti-flute for some reason.
I guessed I would know more when I saw where she brought the flute.
If only I had been aware, as I watched her, that something was watching me...

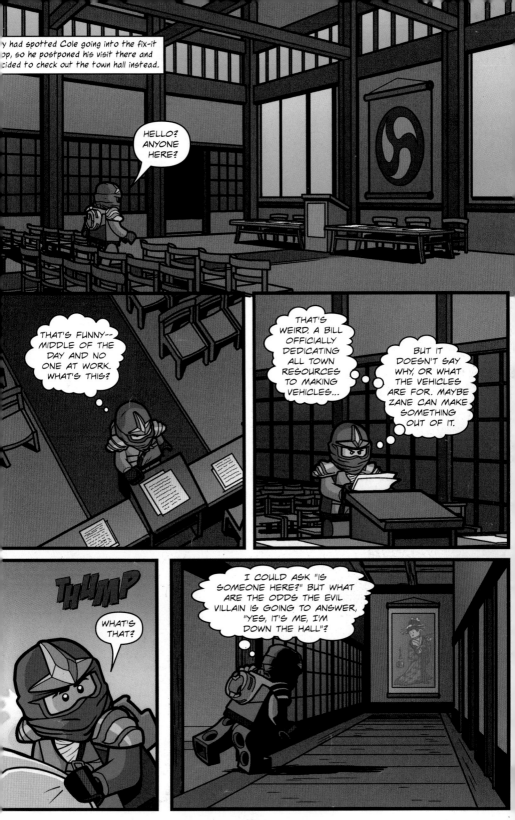

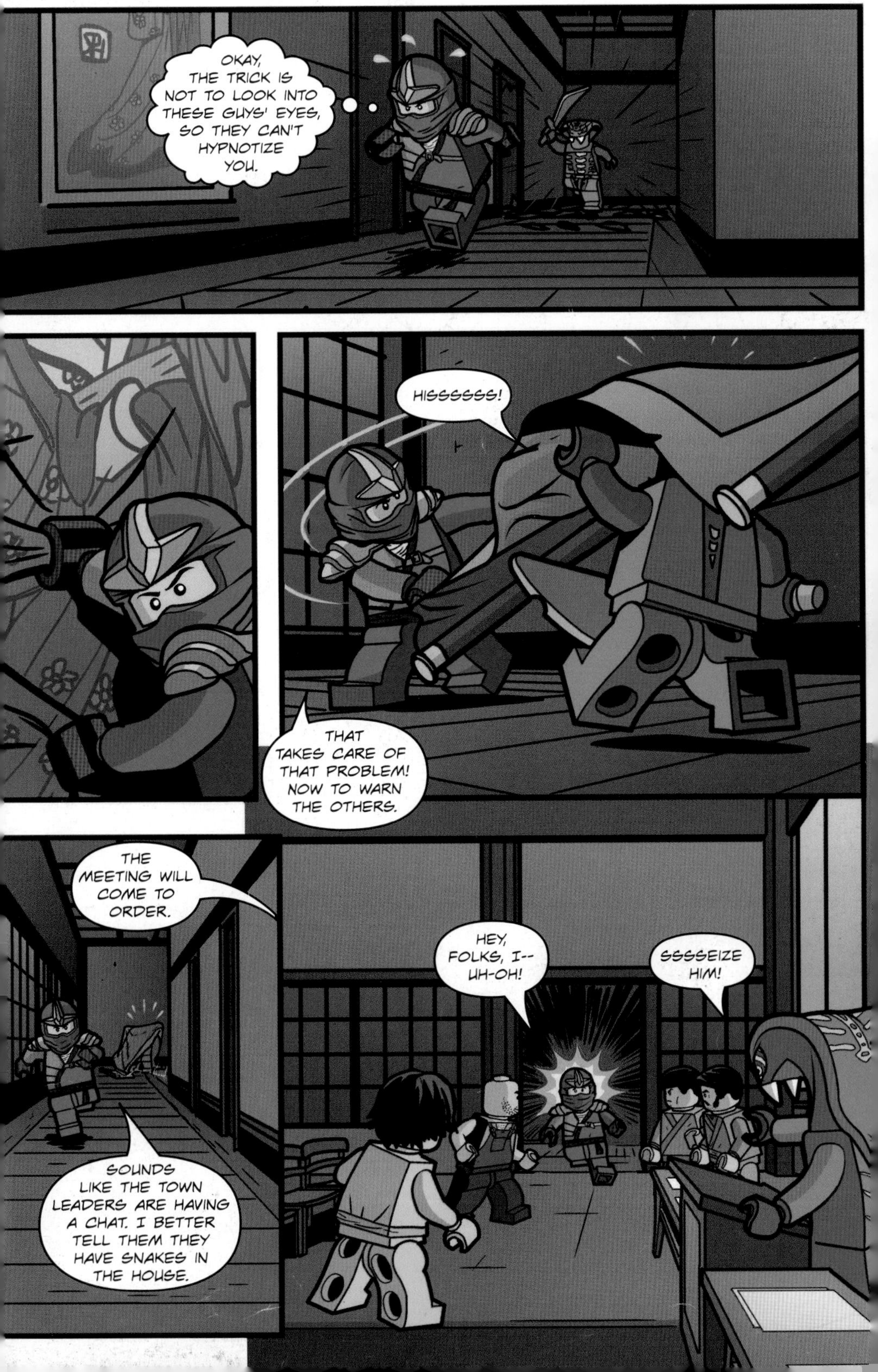
OKAY, THE TRICK IS NOT TO LOOK INTO THESE GUYS' EYES, SO THEY CAN'T HYPNOTIZE YOU.
HISSSSSS!
THAT TAKES CARE OF THAT PROBLEM! NOW TO WARN THE OTHERS.
THE MEETING WILL COME TO ORDER.
SOUNDS LIKE THE TOWN LEADERS ARE HAVING A CHAT. I BETTER TELL THEM THEY HAVE SNAKES IN THE HOUSE.
HEY, FOLKS, I-- UH-OH!
SSSSEIZE HIM!

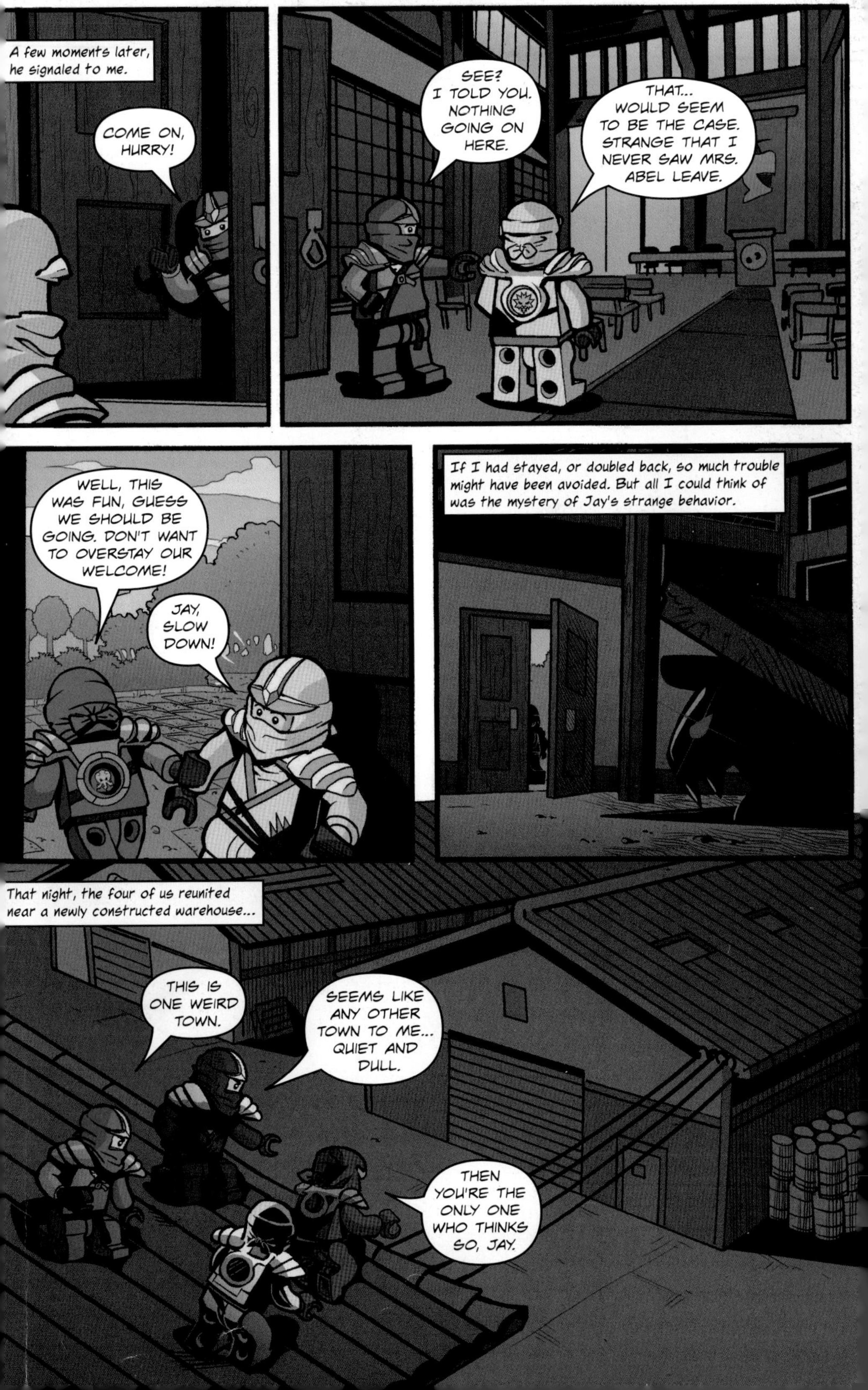
A few moments later, he signaled to me.
COME ON, HURRY!
SEE? I TOLD YOU. NOTHING GOING ON HERE.
THAT... WOULD SEEM TO BE THE CASE. STRANGE THAT I NEVER SAW MRS. ABEL LEAVE.
WELL, THIS WAS FUN, GUESS WE SHOULD BE GOING. DON'T WANT TO OVERSTAY OUR WELCOME!
JAY, SLOW DOWN!
If I had stayed, or doubled back, so much trouble might have been avoided. But all I could think of was the mystery of Jay's strange behavior.
That night, the four of us reunited near a newly constructed warehouse...
THIS IS ONE WEIRD TOWN.
SEEMS LIKE ANY OTHER TOWN TO ME... QUIET AND DULL.
THEN YOU'RE THE ONLY ONE WHO THINKS SO, JAY.

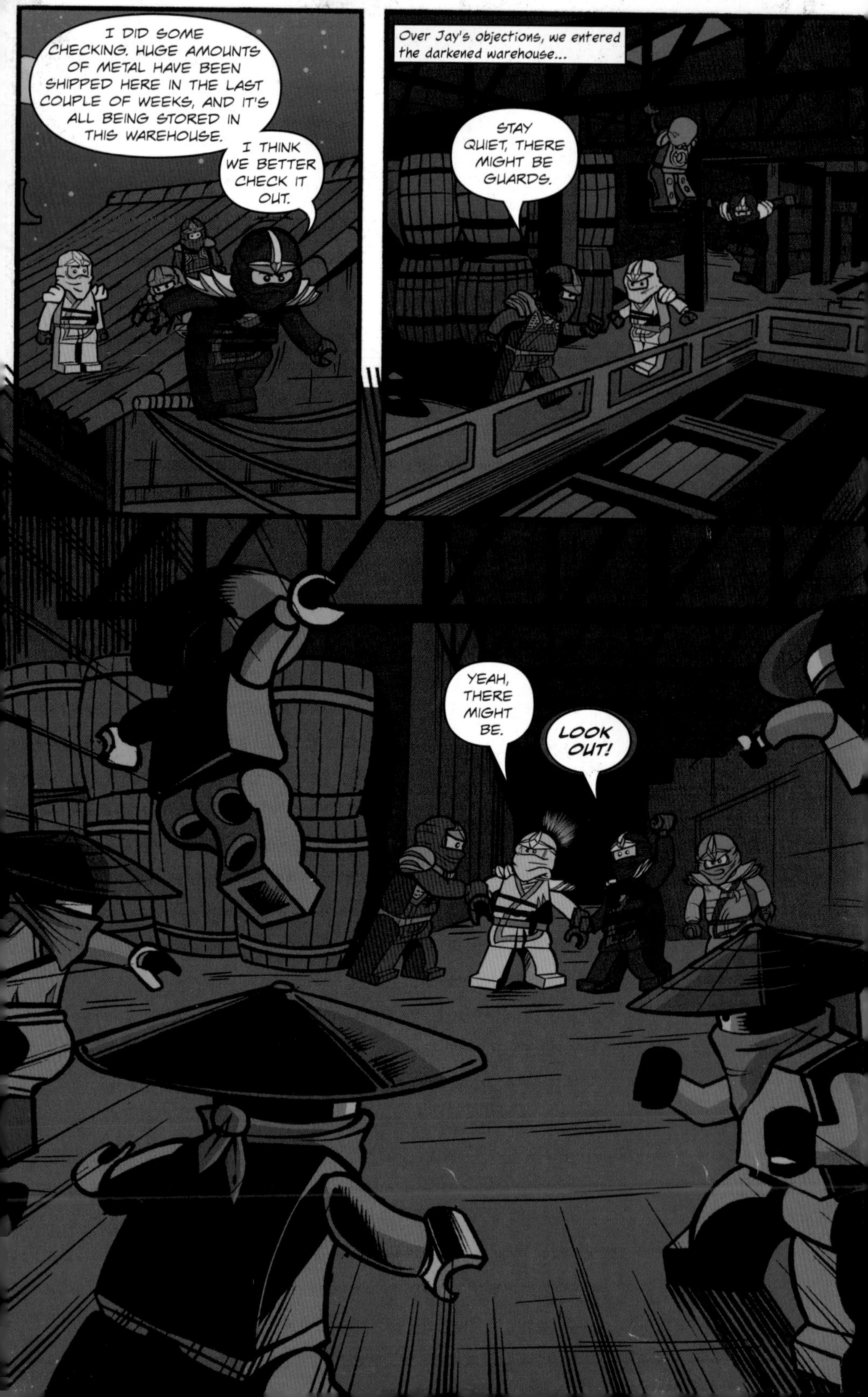
I DID SOME CHECKING. HUGE AMOUNTS OF METAL HAVE BEEN SHIPPED HERE IN THE LAST COUPLE OF WEEKS, AND IT'S ALL BEING STORED IN THIS WAREHOUSE.
I THINK WE BETTER CHECK IT OUT.
Over Jay's objections, we entered the darkened warehouse...
STAY QUIET, THERE MIGHT BE GUARDS.
YEAH, THERE MIGHT BE.
LOOK OUT!

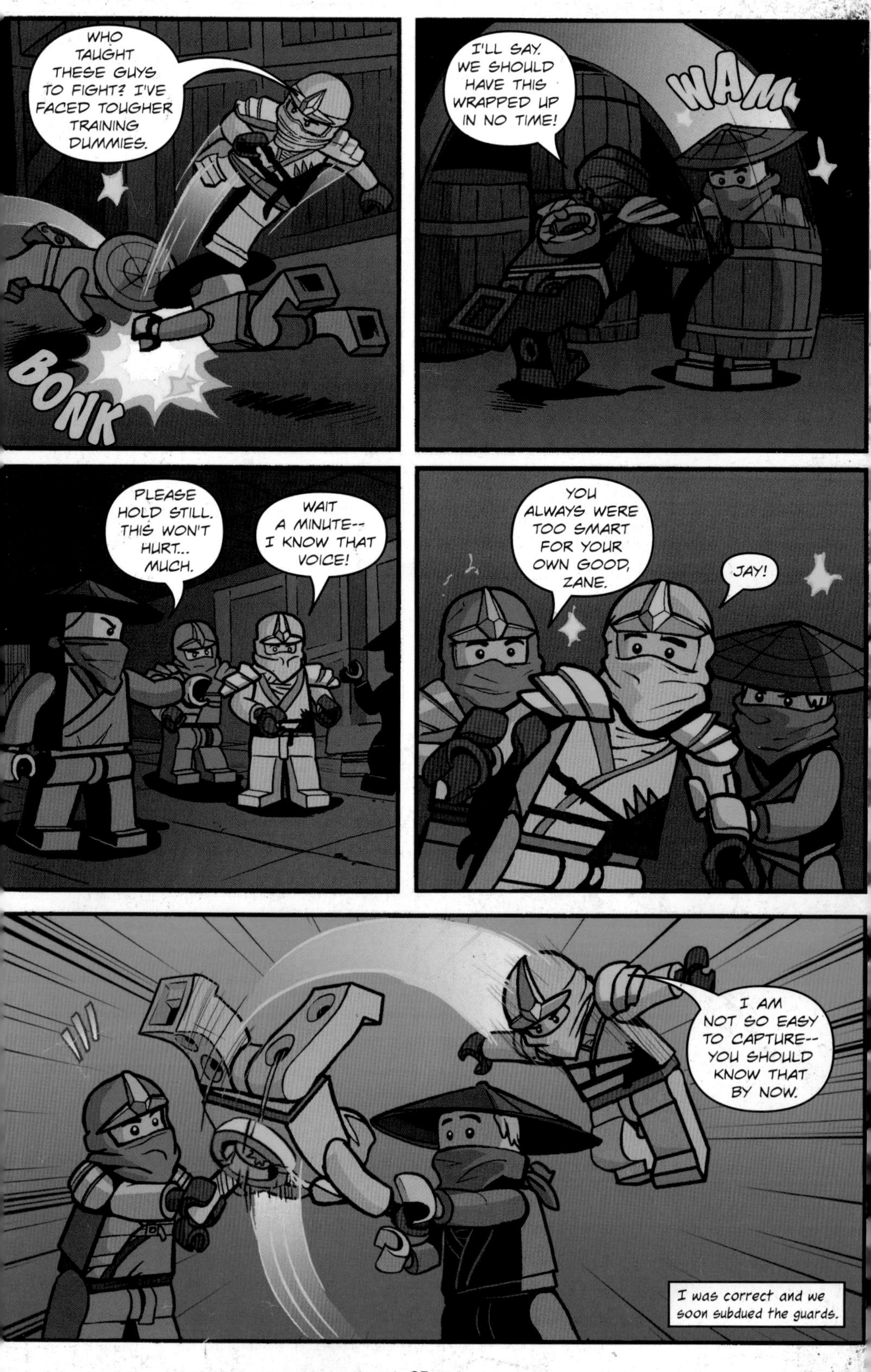
WHO TAUGHT THESE GUYS TO FIGHT? I'VE FACED TOUGHER TRAINING DUMMIES.
BONK
I'LL SAY. WE SHOULD HAVE THIS WRAPPED UP IN NO TIME!
WAM
PLEASE HOLD STILL. THIS WON'T HURT... MUCH.
WAIT A MINUTE-- I KNOW THAT VOICE!
YOU ALWAYS WERE TOO SMART FOR YOUR OWN GOOD, ZANE.
JAY!
I AM NOT SO EASY TO CAPTURE-- YOU SHOULD KNOW THAT BY NOW.
I was correct and we soon subdued the guards.

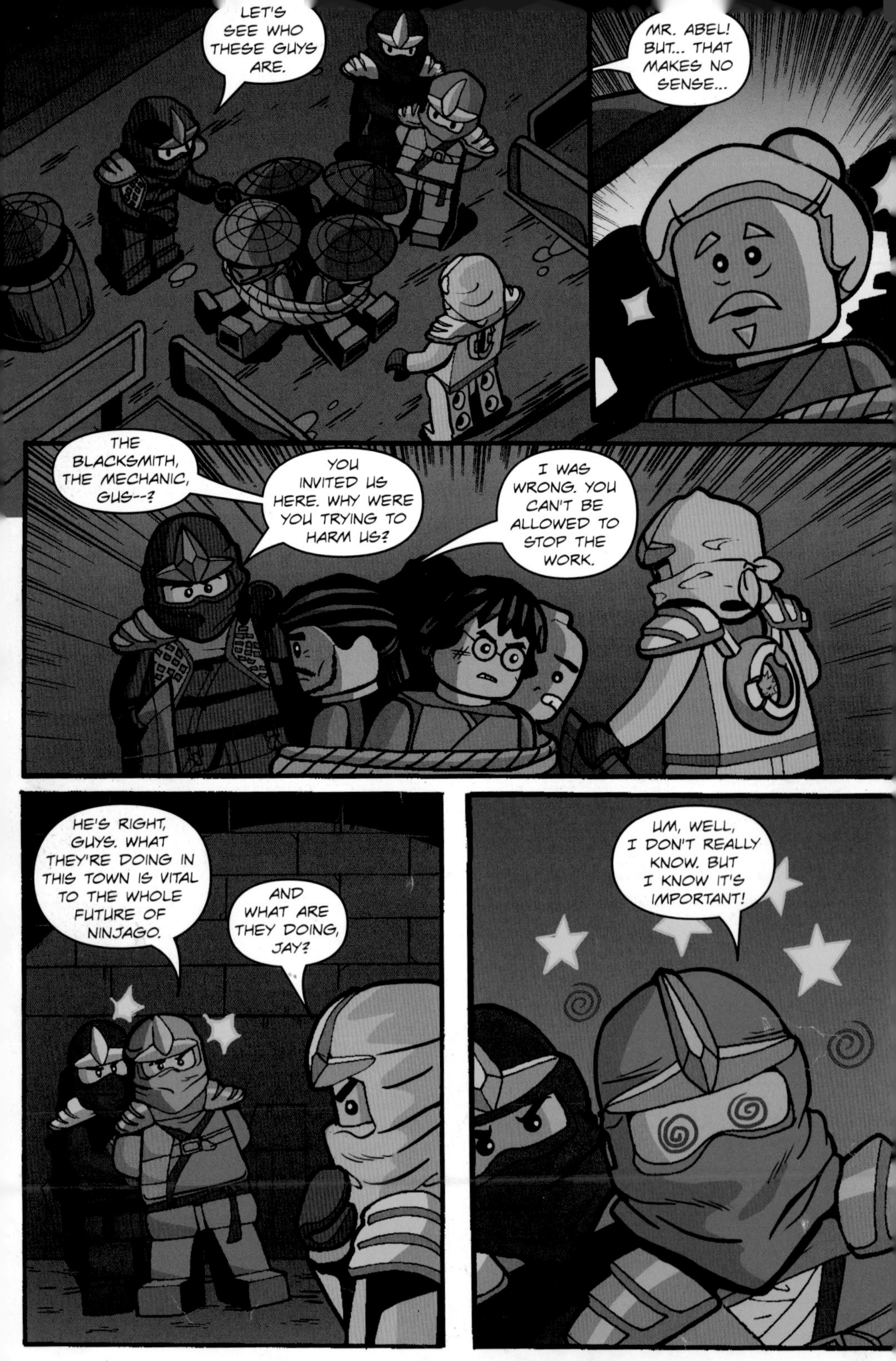
LET'S SEE WHO THESE GUYS ARE.
MR. ABEL! BUT... THAT MAKES NO SENSE...
THE BLACKSMITH, THE MECHANIC, GUS--?
YOU INVITED US HERE. WHY WERE YOU TRYING TO HARM US?
I WAS WRONG. YOU CAN'T BE ALLOWED TO STOP THE WORK.
HE'S RIGHT, GUYS. WHAT THEY'RE DOING IN THIS TOWN IS VITAL TO THE WHOLE FUTURE OF NINJAGO.
AND WHAT ARE THEY DOING, JAY?
UM, WELL, I DON'T REALLY KNOW. BUT I KNOW IT'S IMPORTANT!

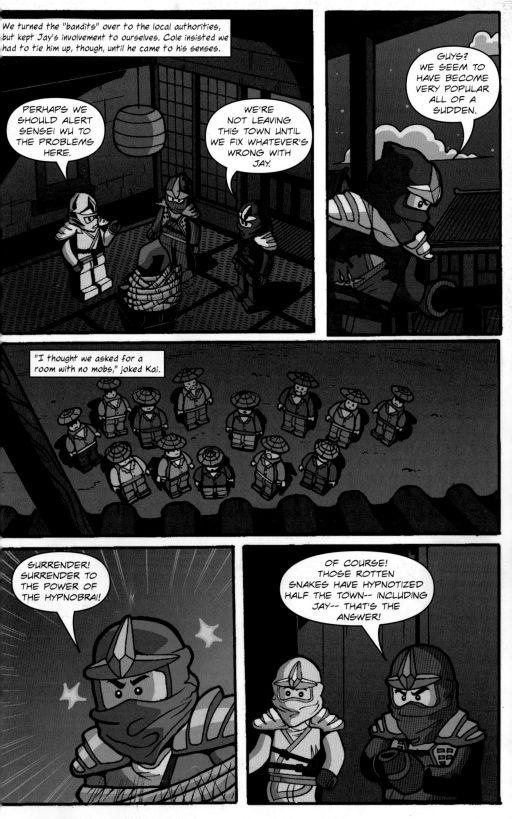

We turned the "bandits" over to the local authorities, but kept Jay's involvement to ourselves. Cole insisted we had to tie him up, though, until he came to his senses.

PERHAPS WE SHOULD ALERT SENSEI WU TO THE PROBLEMS HERE.

WE'RE NOT LEAVING THIS TOWN UNTIL WE FIX WHATEVER'S WRONG WITH JAY.

GUYS? WE SEEM TO HAVE BECOME VERY POPULAR ALL OF A SUDDEN.

"I thought we asked for a room with no mobs," joked Kai.

SURRENDER! SURRENDER TO THE POWER OF THE HYPNOBRAI!

OF COURSE! THOSE ROTTEN SNAKES HAVE HYPNOTIZED HALF THE TOWN-- INCLUDING JAY-- THAT'S THE ANSWER!

27

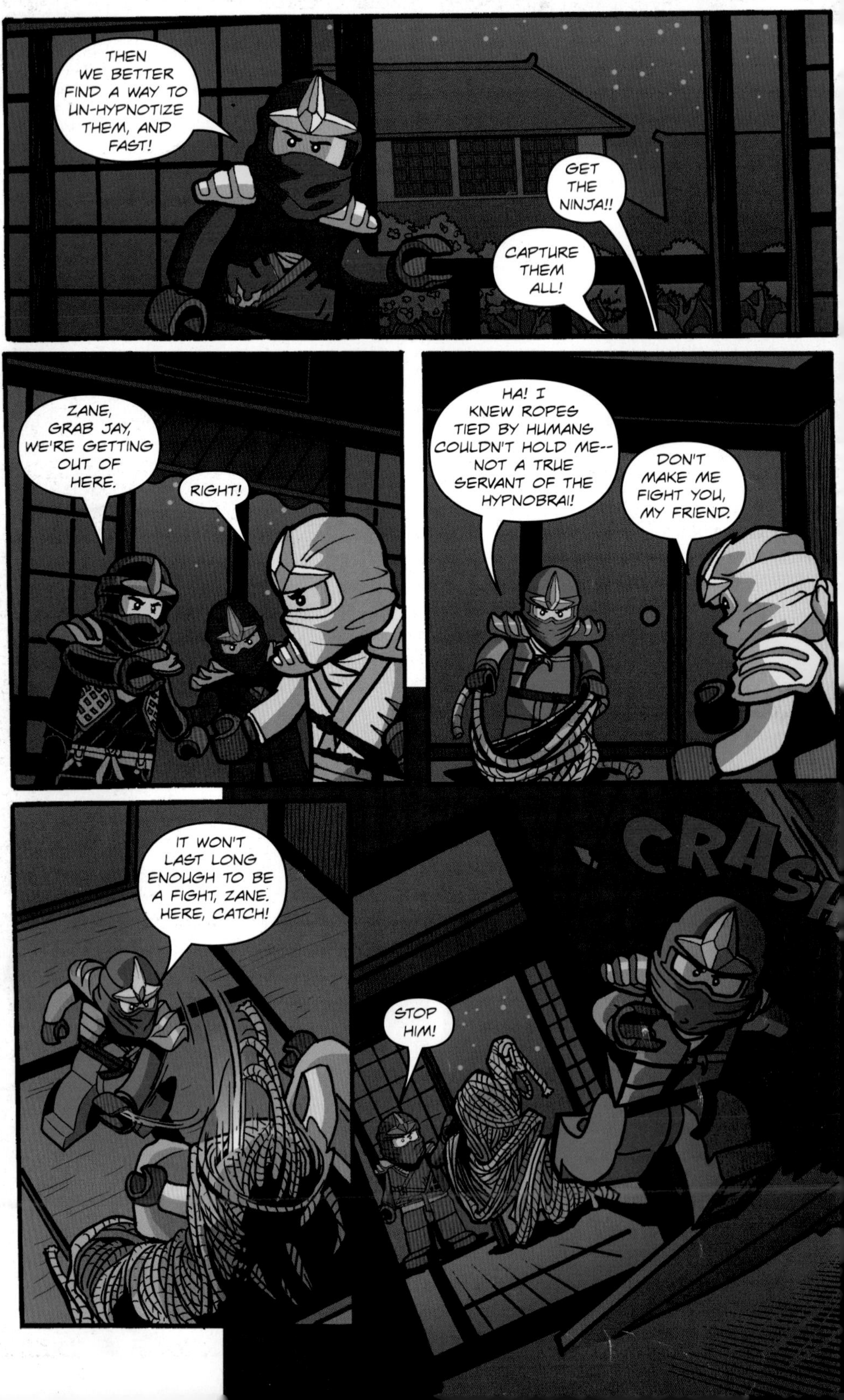
THEN WE BETTER FIND A WAY TO UN-HYPNOTIZE THEM, AND FAST!
GET THE NINJA!!
CAPTURE THEM ALL!
ZANE, GRAB JAY, WE'RE GETTING OUT OF HERE.
RIGHT!
HA! I KNEW ROPES TIED BY HUMANS COULDN'T HOLD ME-- NOT A TRUE SERVANT OF THE HYPNOBRAI!
DON'T MAKE ME FIGHT YOU, MY FRIEND.
IT WON'T LAST LONG ENOUGH TO BE A FIGHT, ZANE. HERE, CATCH!
CRASH
STOP HIM!

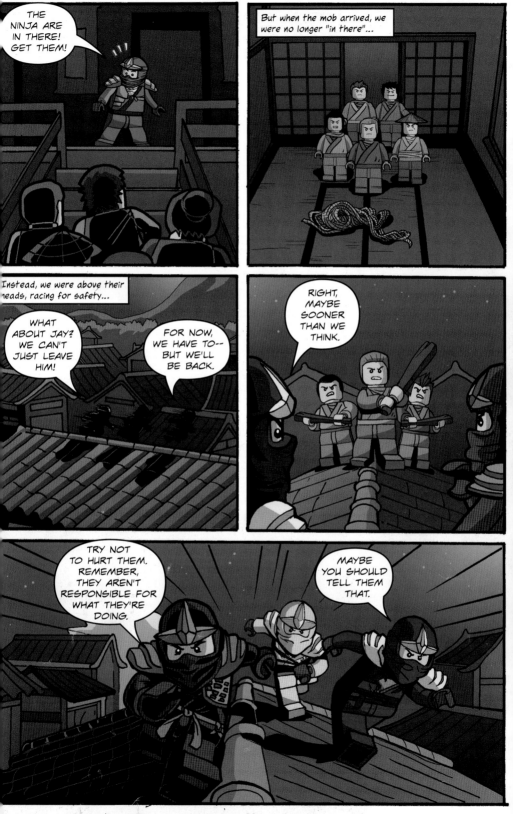

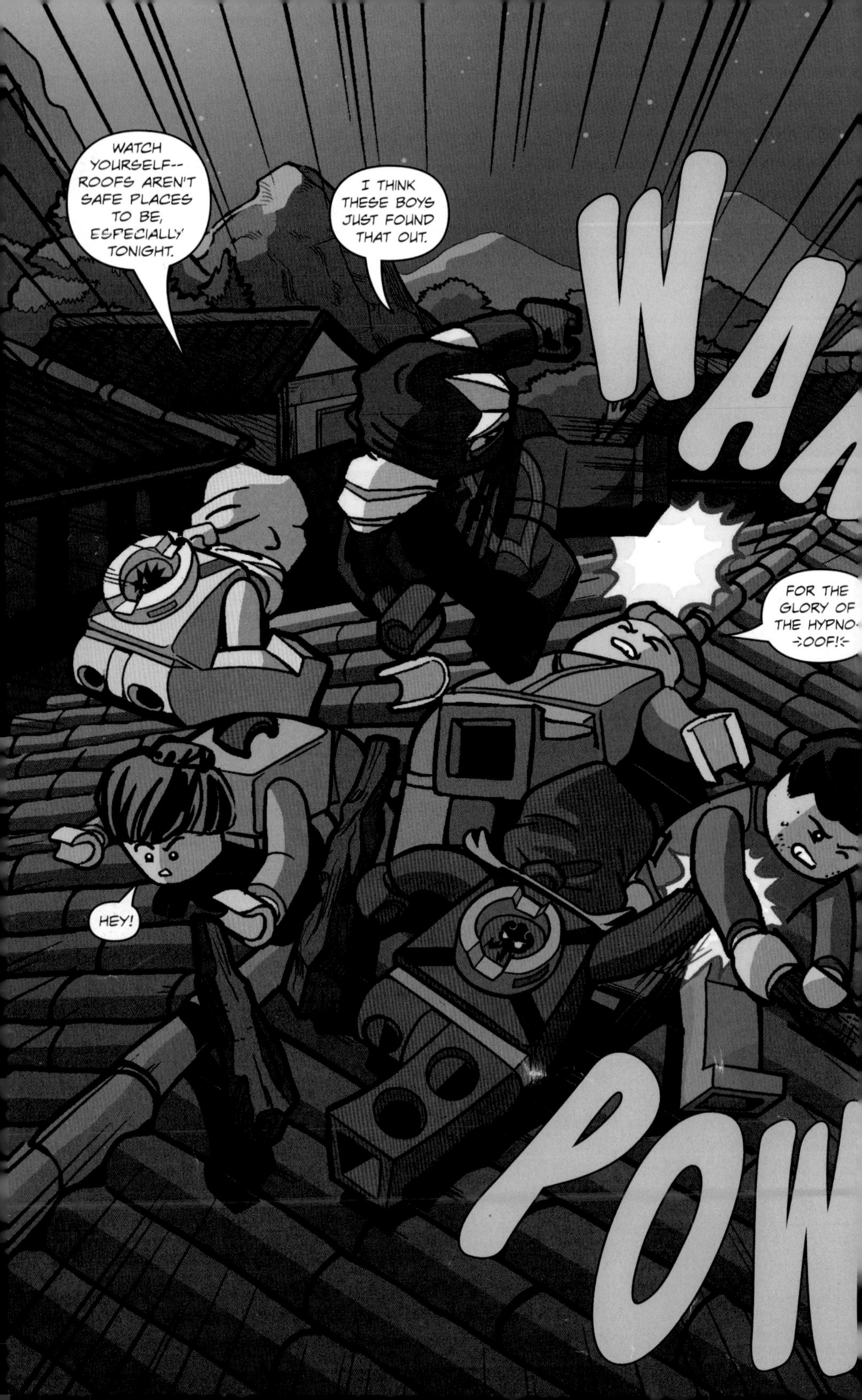
WATCH YOURSELF-- ROOFS AREN'T SAFE PLACES TO BE, ESPECIALLY TONIGHT.
I THINK THESE BOYS JUST FOUND THAT OUT.
FOR THE GLORY OF THE HYPNO- -OOF!
HEY!

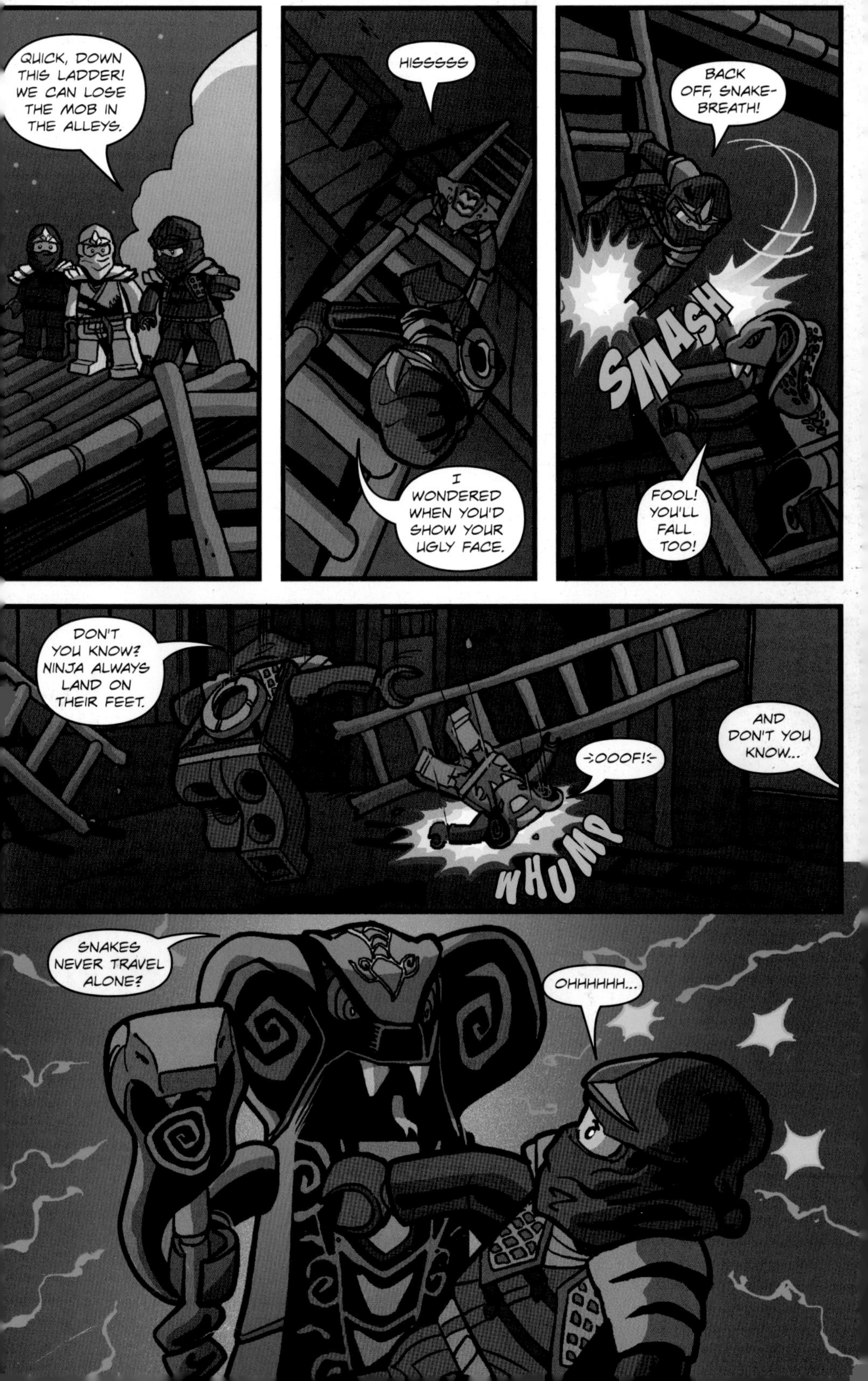
QUICK, DOWN THIS LADDER! WE CAN LOSE THE MOB IN THE ALLEYS.
HISSSSS
I WONDERED WHEN YOU'D SHOW YOUR UGLY FACE.
BACK OFF, SNAKE-BREATH!
SMASH
FOOL! YOU'LL FALL TOO!
DON'T YOU KNOW? NINJA ALWAYS LAND ON THEIR FEET.
OOOF!
WHUMP
AND DON'T YOU KNOW...
SNAKES NEVER TRAVEL ALONE?
OHHHHHH...

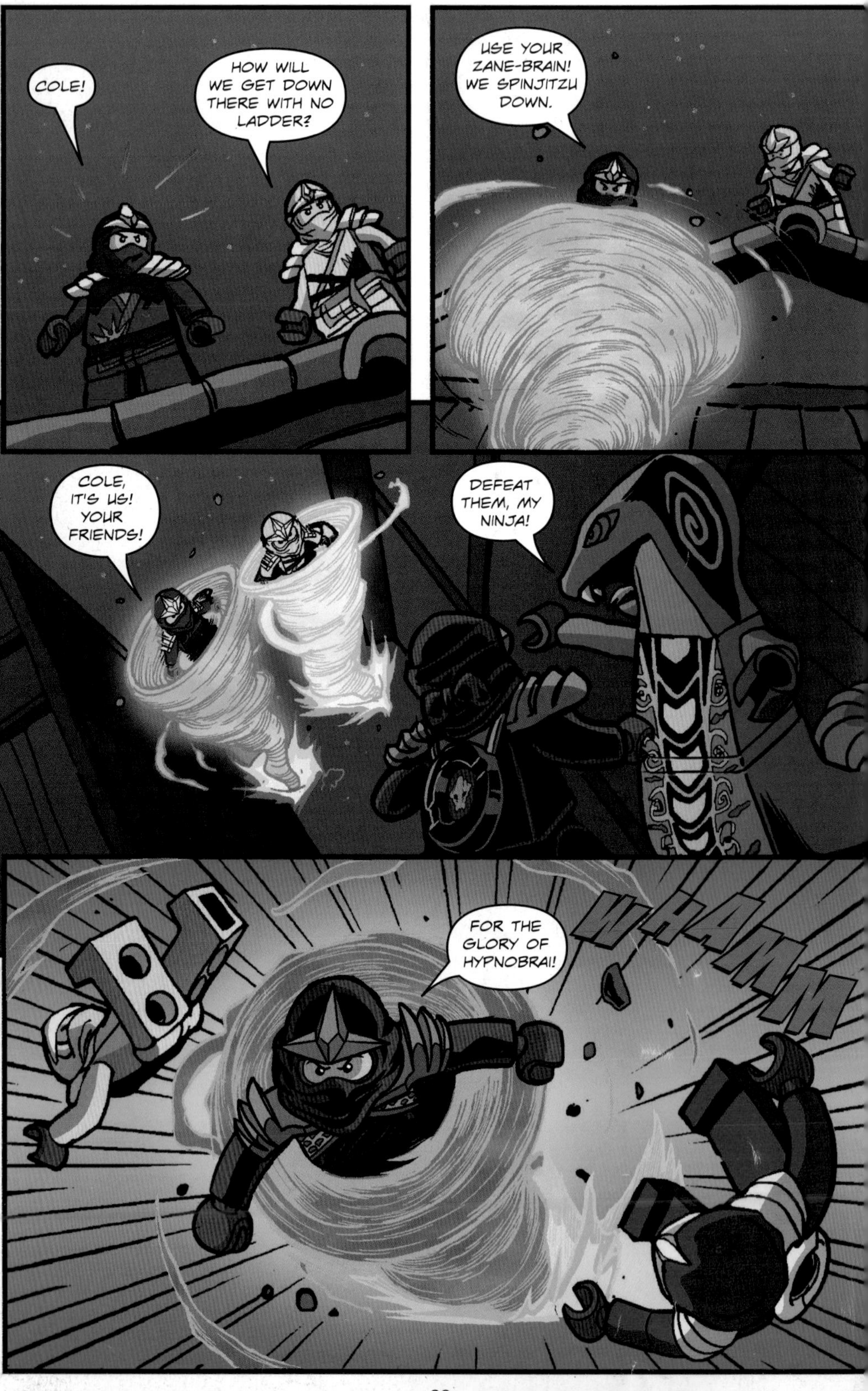
COLE!
HOW WILL WE GET DOWN THERE WITH NO LADDER?
USE YOUR ZANE-BRAIN! WE SPINJITZU DOWN.
COLE, IT'S US! YOUR FRIENDS!
DEFEAT THEM, MY NINJA!
FOR THE GLORY OF HYPNOBRAI!
WHAMM

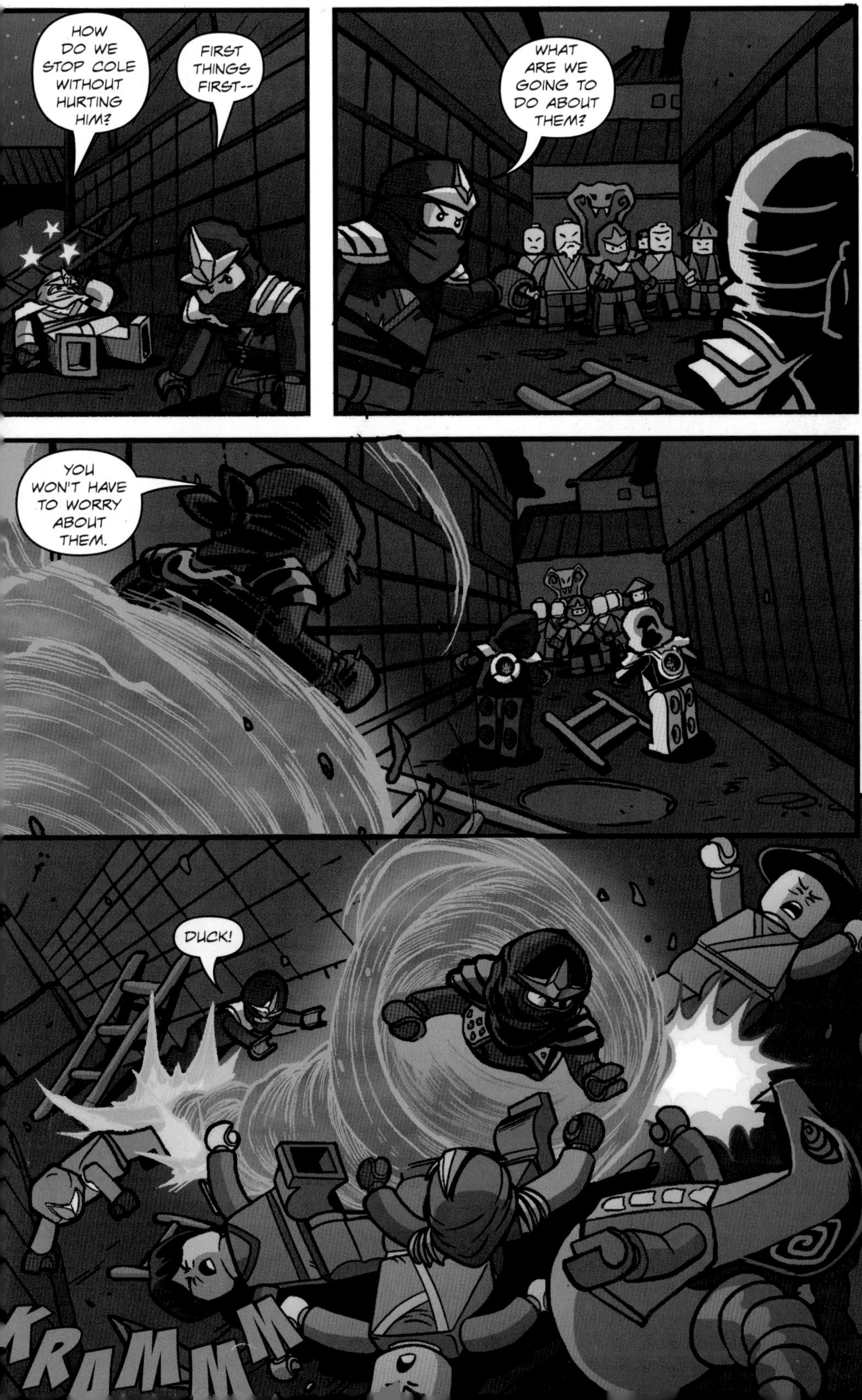
HOW DO WE STOP COLE WITHOUT HURTING HIM?
FIRST THINGS FIRST--
WHAT ARE WE GOING TO DO ABOUT THEM?
YOU WON'T HAVE TO WORRY ABOUT THEM.
DUCK!
KRAMMM

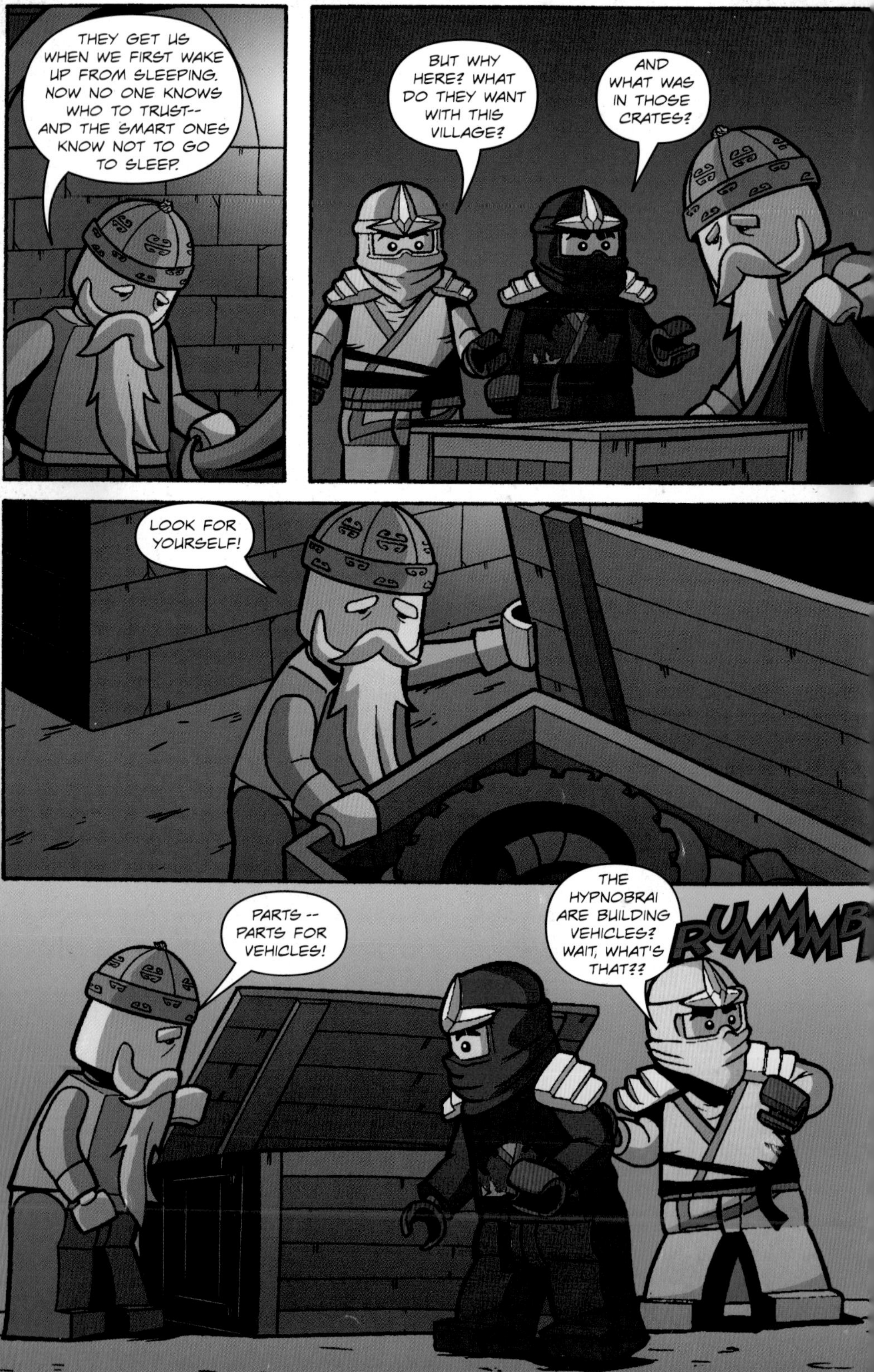
THEY GET US WHEN WE FIRST WAKE UP FROM SLEEPING. NOW NO ONE KNOWS WHO TO TRUST-- AND THE SMART ONES KNOW NOT TO GO TO SLEEP.
BUT WHY HERE? WHAT DO THEY WANT WITH THIS VILLAGE?
AND WHAT WAS IN THOSE CRATES?
LOOK FOR YOURSELF!
PARTS -- PARTS FOR VEHICLES!
THE HYPNOBRAI ARE BUILDING VEHICLES? WAIT, WHAT'S THAT??
RUMMMB

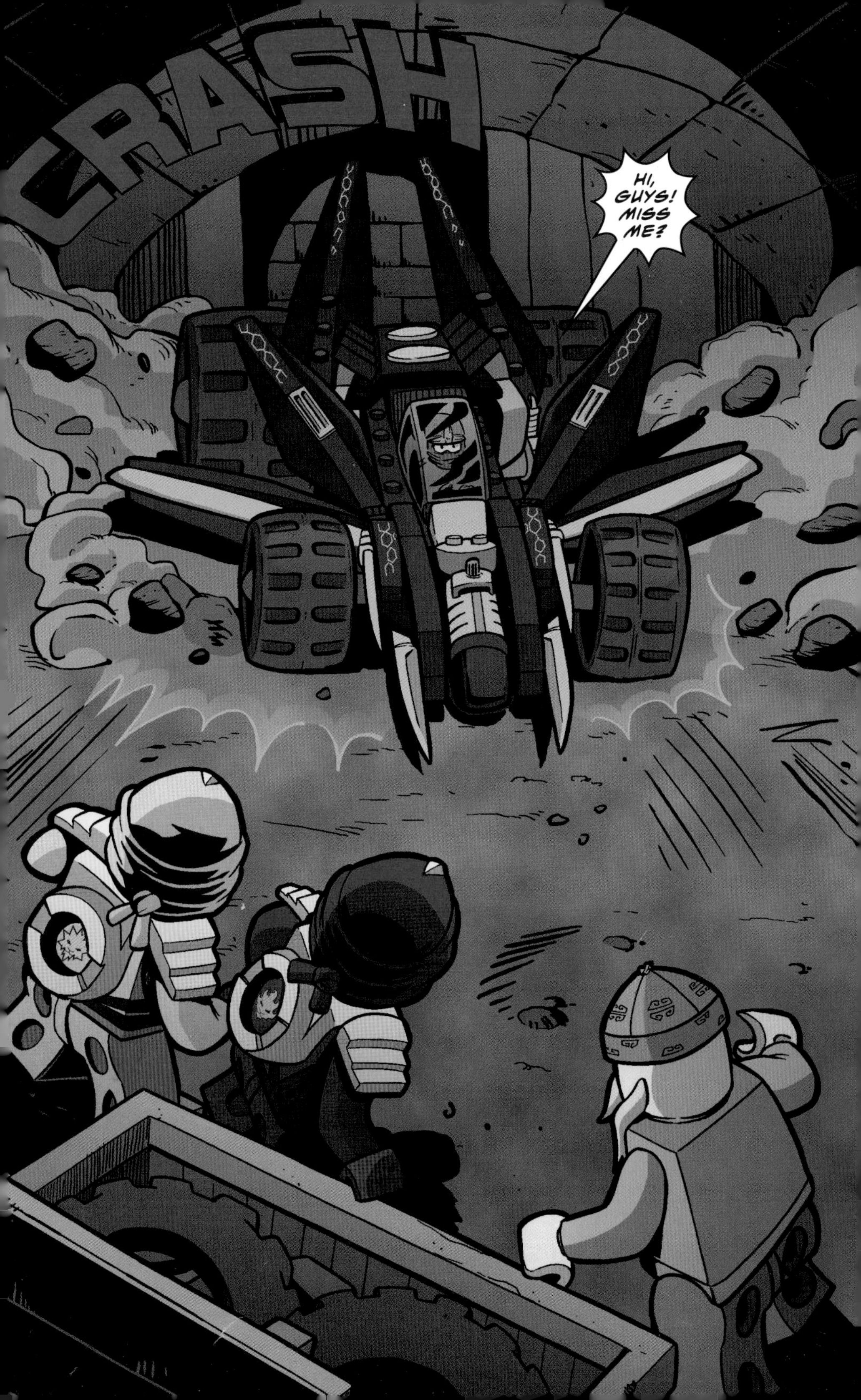
CRASH
HI, GUYS! MISS ME?

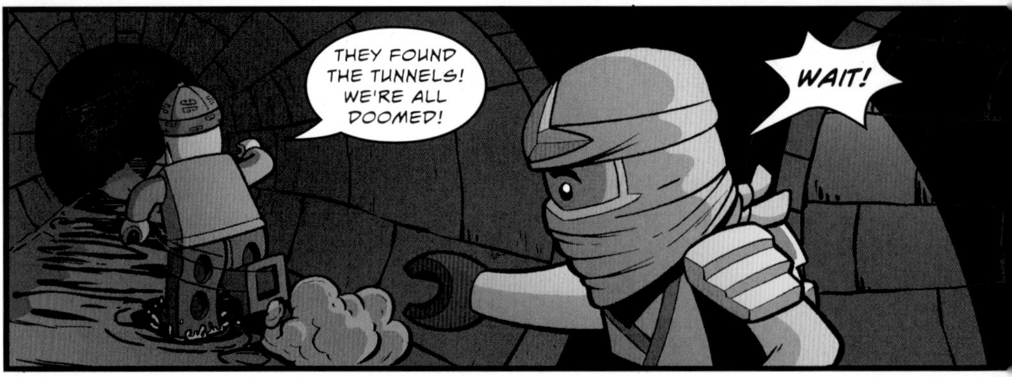
THEY FOUND THE TUNNELS! WE'RE ALL DOOMED!
WAIT!

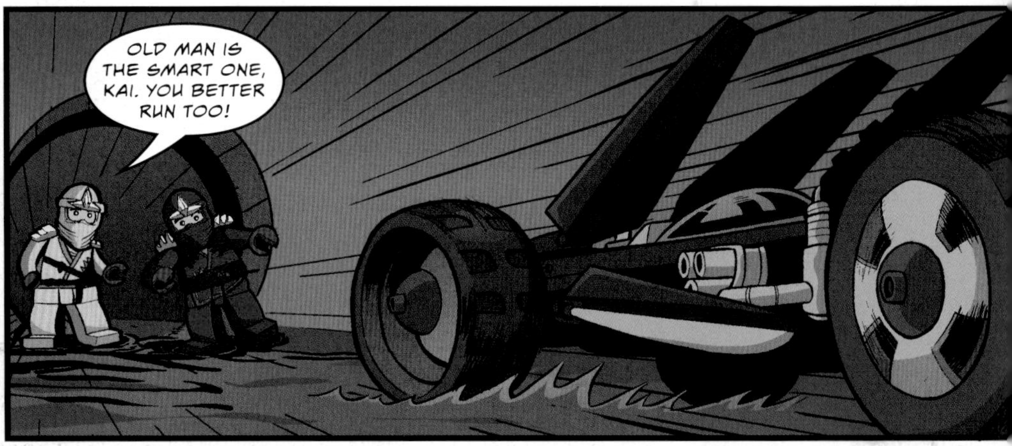
OLD MAN IS THE SMART ONE, KAI. YOU BETTER RUN TOO!

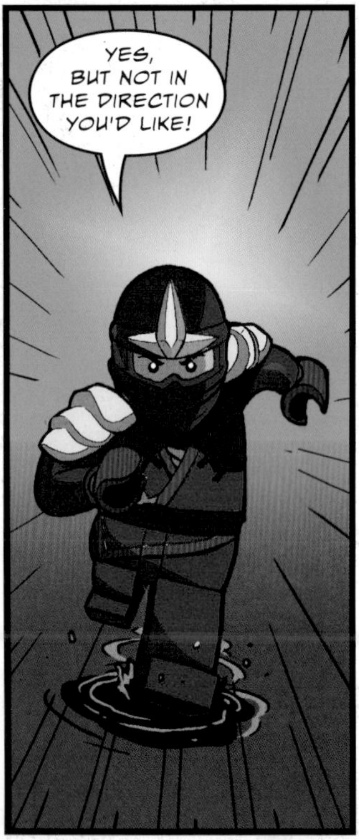
YES, BUT NOT IN THE DIRECTION YOU'D LIKE!

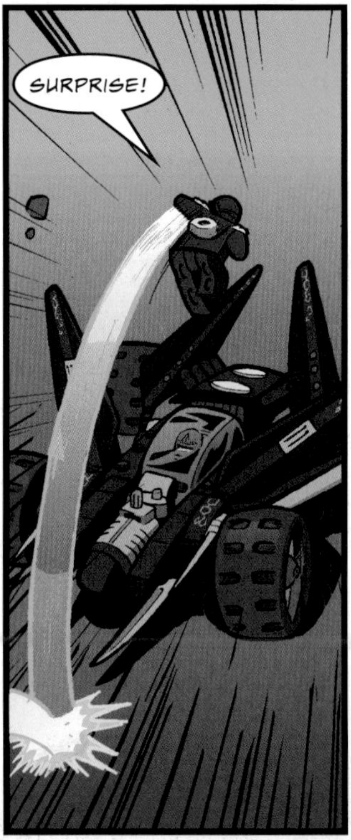
SURPRISE!

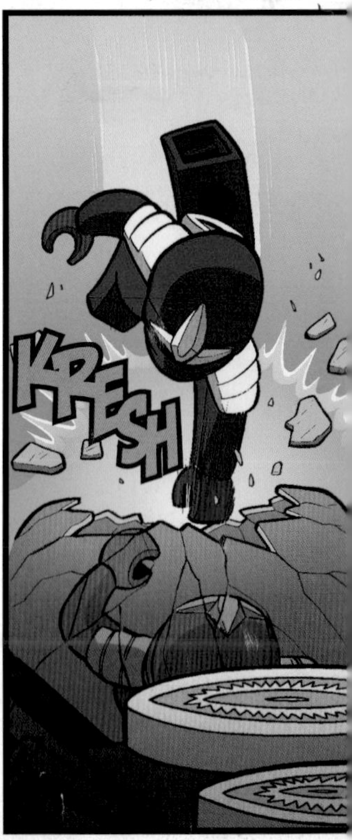
KRESH

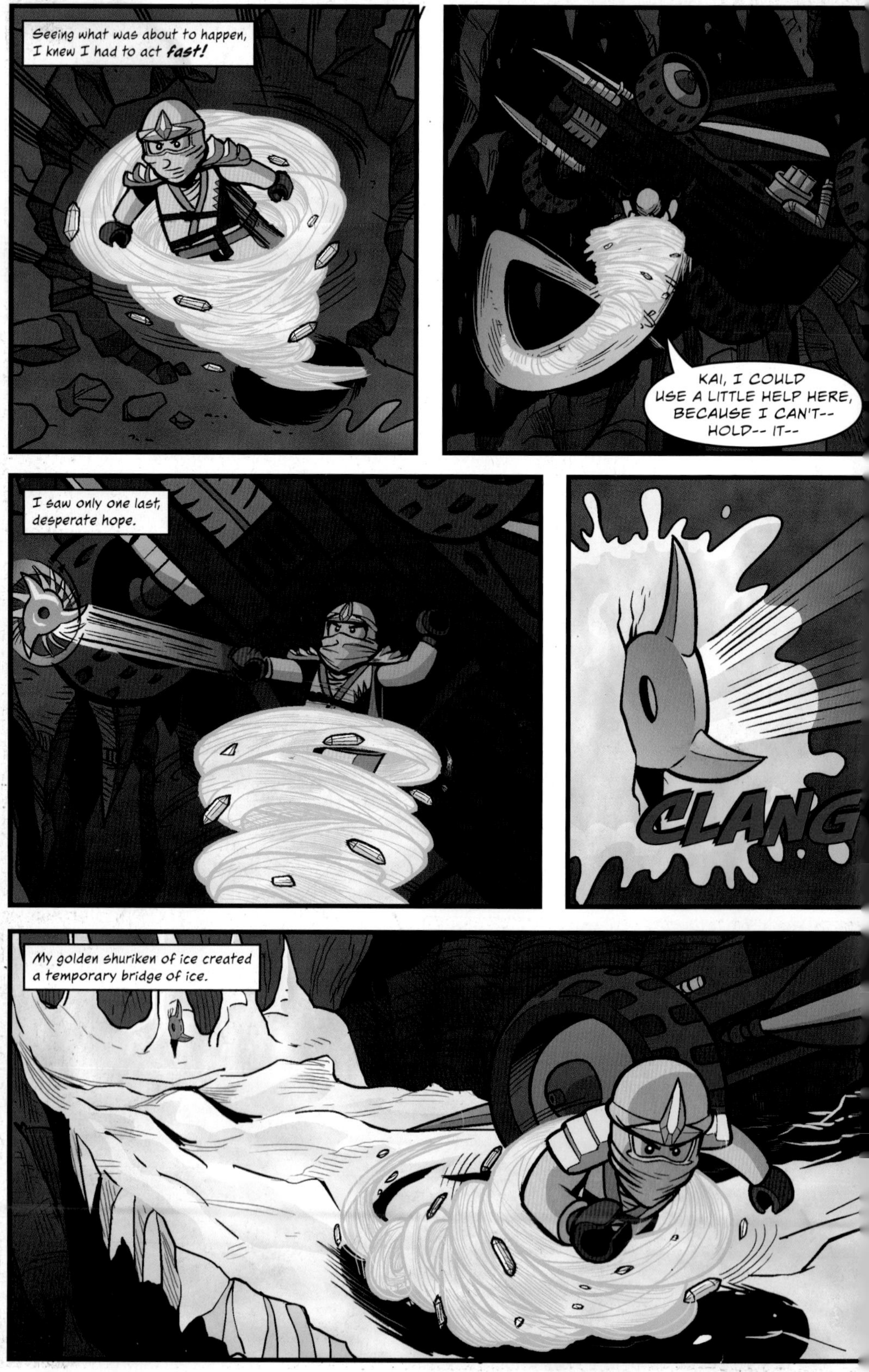
Seeing what was about to happen, I knew I had to act **fast!**
KAI, I COULD USE A LITTLE HELP HERE, BECAUSE I CAN'T-- HOLD-- IT--
I saw only one last, desperate hope.
CLANG
My golden shuriken of ice created a temporary bridge of ice.

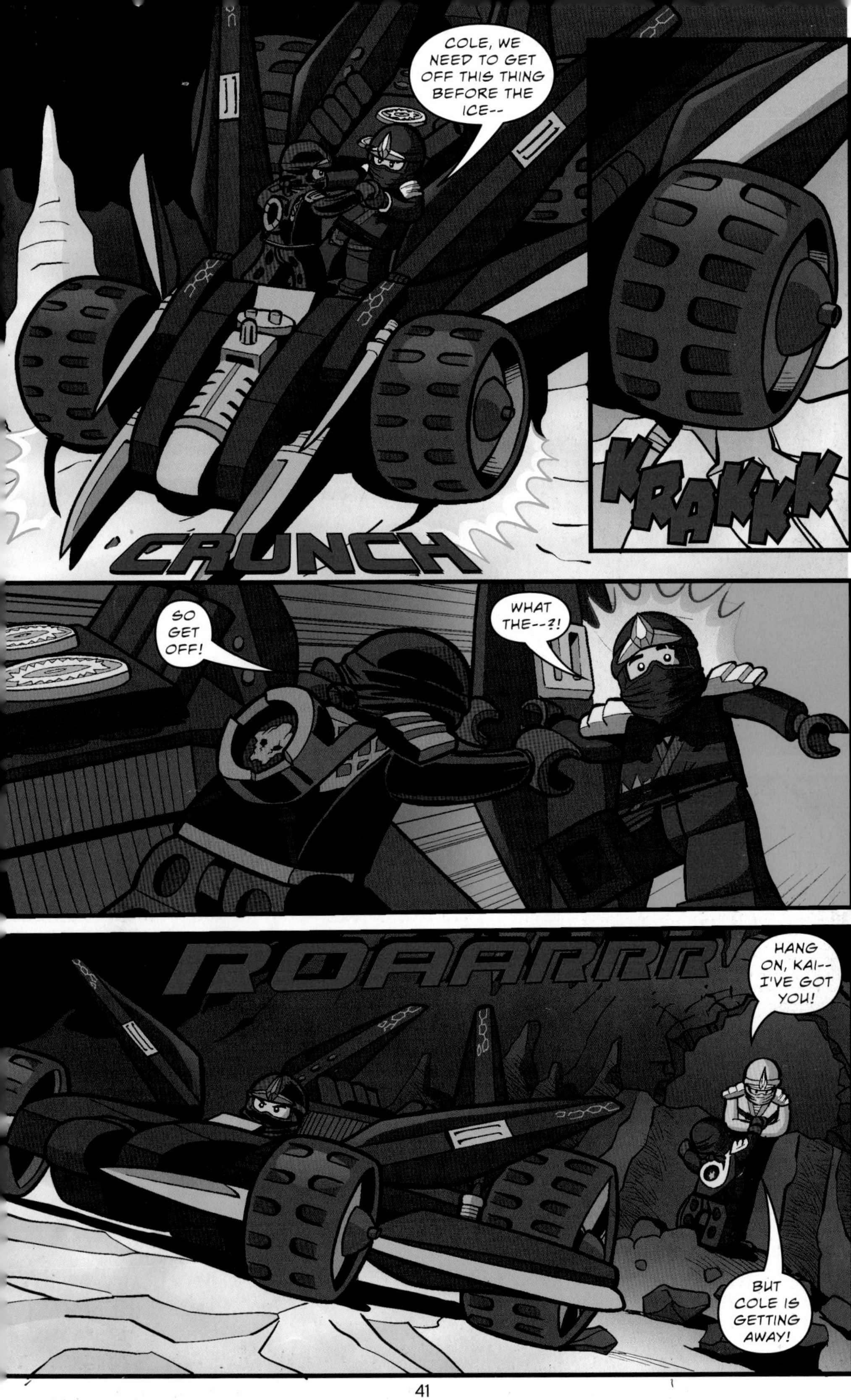
COLE, WE NEED TO GET OFF THIS THING BEFORE THE ICE--
CRUNCH
KRAKKK
SO GET OFF!
WHAT THE--?!
ROAARRR
HANG ON, KAI-- I'VE GOT YOU!
BUT COLE IS GETTING AWAY!

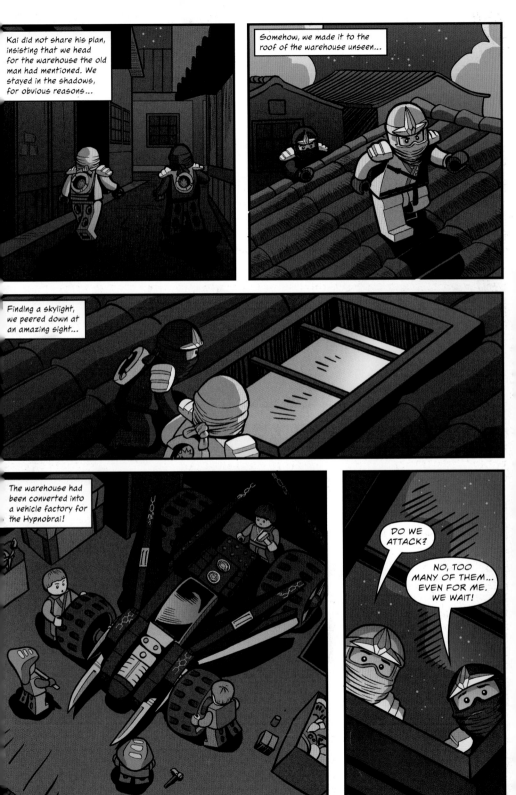

Kai did not share his plan, insisting that we head for the warehouse the old man had mentioned. We stayed in the shadows, for obvious reasons...

Somehow, we made it to the roof of the warehouse unseen...

Finding a skylight, we peered down at an amazing sight...

The warehouse had been converted into a vehicle factory for the Hypnobrai!

DO WE ATTACK?

NO, TOO MANY OF THEM... EVEN FOR ME. WE WAIT!

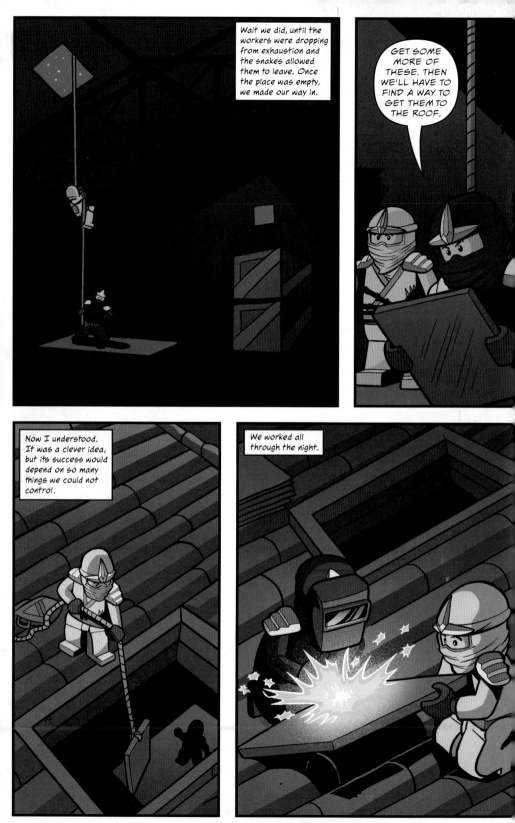

Wait we did, until the workers were dropping from exhaustion and the snakes allowed them to leave. Once the place was empty, we made our way in.

GET SOME MORE OF THESE. THEN WE'LL HAVE TO FIND A WAY TO GET THEM TO THE ROOF.

Now I understood. It was a clever idea, but its success would depend on so many things we could not control.

We worked all through the night.

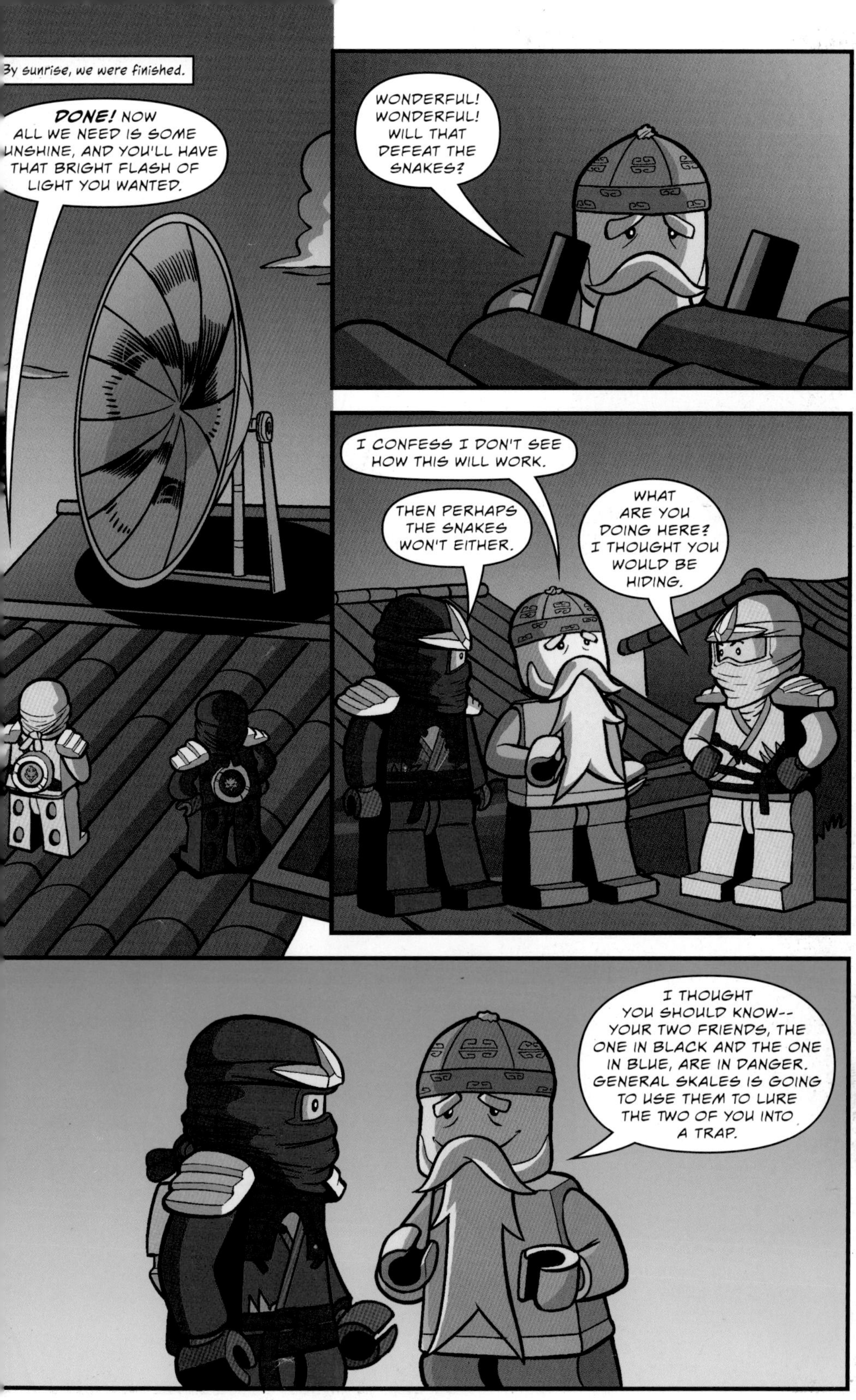
y sunrise, we were finished.
DONE! NOW ALL WE NEED IS SOME UNSHINE, AND YOU'LL HAVE THAT BRIGHT FLASH OF LIGHT YOU WANTED.
WONDERFUL! WONDERFUL! WILL THAT DEFEAT THE SNAKES?
I CONFESS I DON'T SEE HOW THIS WILL WORK.
THEN PERHAPS THE SNAKES WON'T EITHER.
WHAT ARE YOU DOING HERE? I THOUGHT YOU WOULD BE HIDING.
I THOUGHT YOU SHOULD KNOW-- YOUR TWO FRIENDS, THE ONE IN BLACK AND THE ONE IN BLUE, ARE IN DANGER. GENERAL SKALES IS GOING TO USE THEM TO LURE THE TWO OF YOU INTO A TRAP.

The old man gave us an address, and Kai went with him, telling me to man the reflector.

Left alone, I had time to think about what our new friend had said about our friends, Cole and Jay.

"The one in black and the one in blue" he had called them and... then it struck me.

The old man had seen Cole in the tunnels, but he had never seen Jay. How did he know he wore blue... unless the Hypnobrai had told him?

It was a **trap**, and Kai was walking right into it!

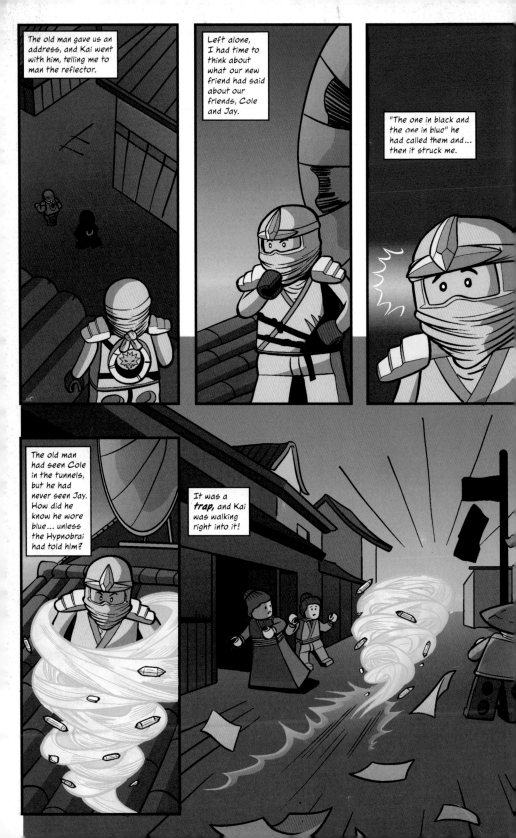

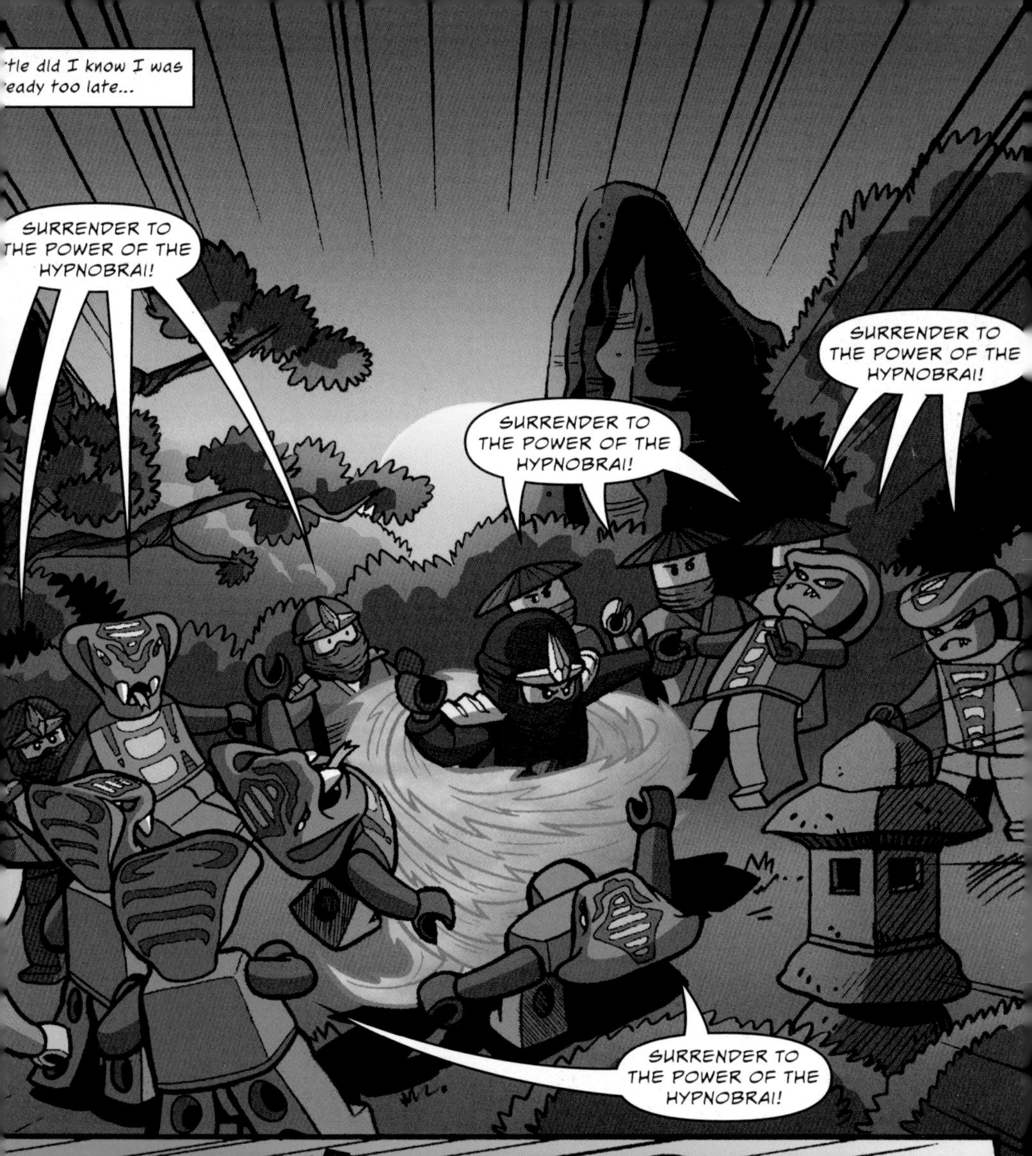

ttle did I know I was
eady too late...
SURRENDER TO THE POWER OF THE HYPNOBRAI!
SURRENDER TO THE POWER OF THE HYPNOBRAI!
SURRENDER TO THE POWER OF THE HYPNOBRAI!
SURRENDER TO THE POWER OF THE HYPNOBRAI!

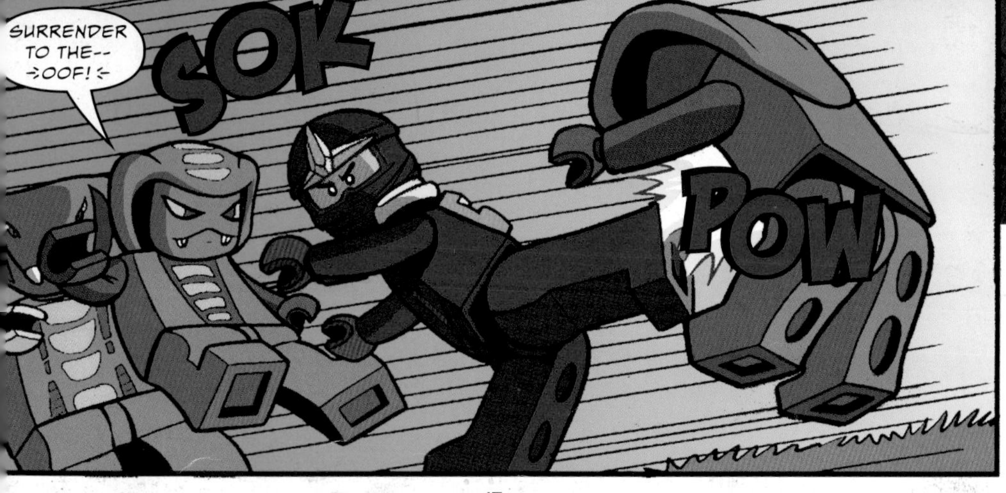

SURRENDER TO THE-- ⇒OOF!⇐
SOK
POW

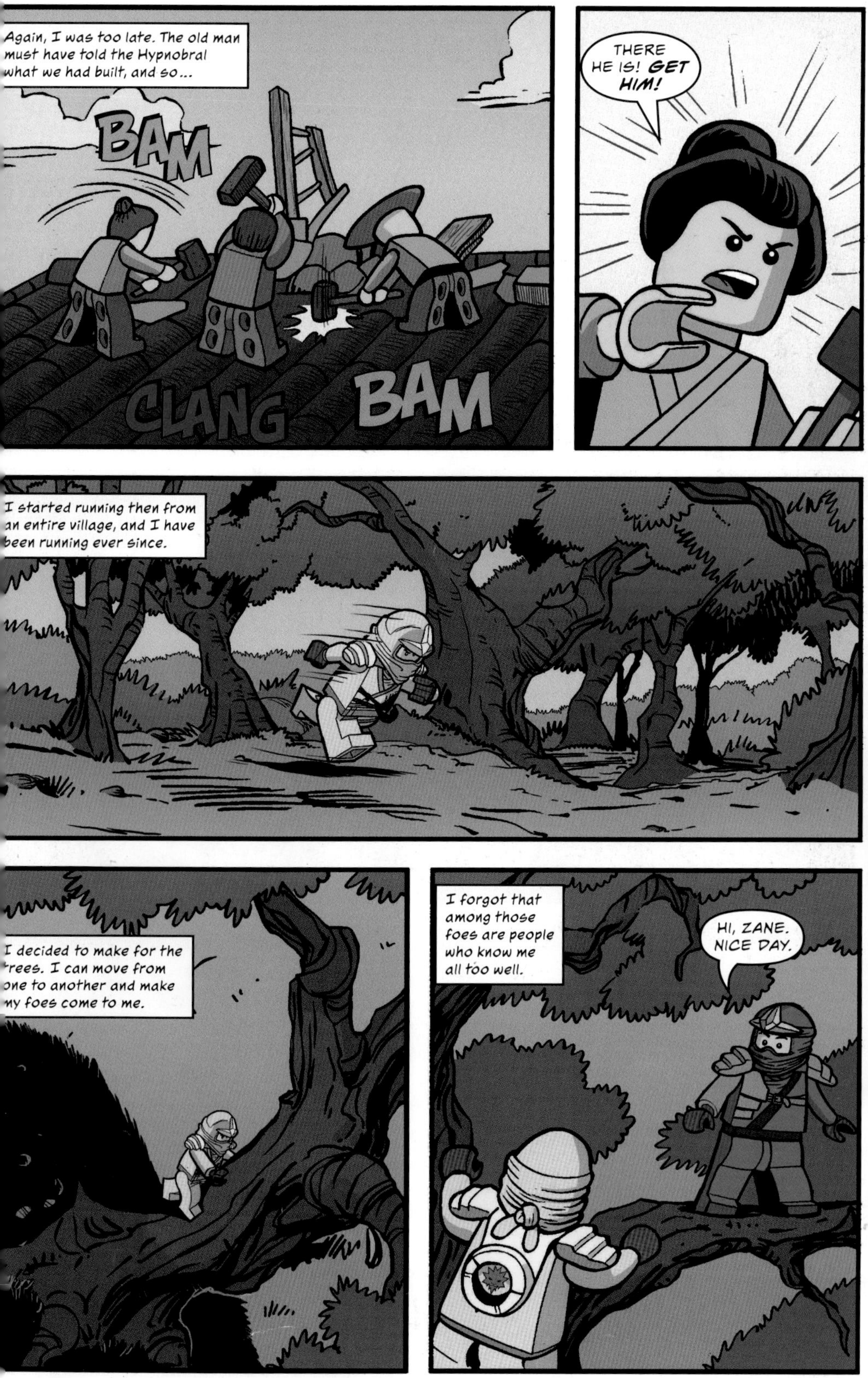
Again, I was too late. The old man must have told the Hypnobrai what we had built, and so...
BAM
CLANG
BAM
THERE HE IS! GET HIM!
I started running then from an entire village, and I have been running ever since.
I decided to make for the trees. I can move from one to another and make my foes come to me.
I forgot that among those foes are people who know me all too well.
HI, ZANE. NICE DAY.

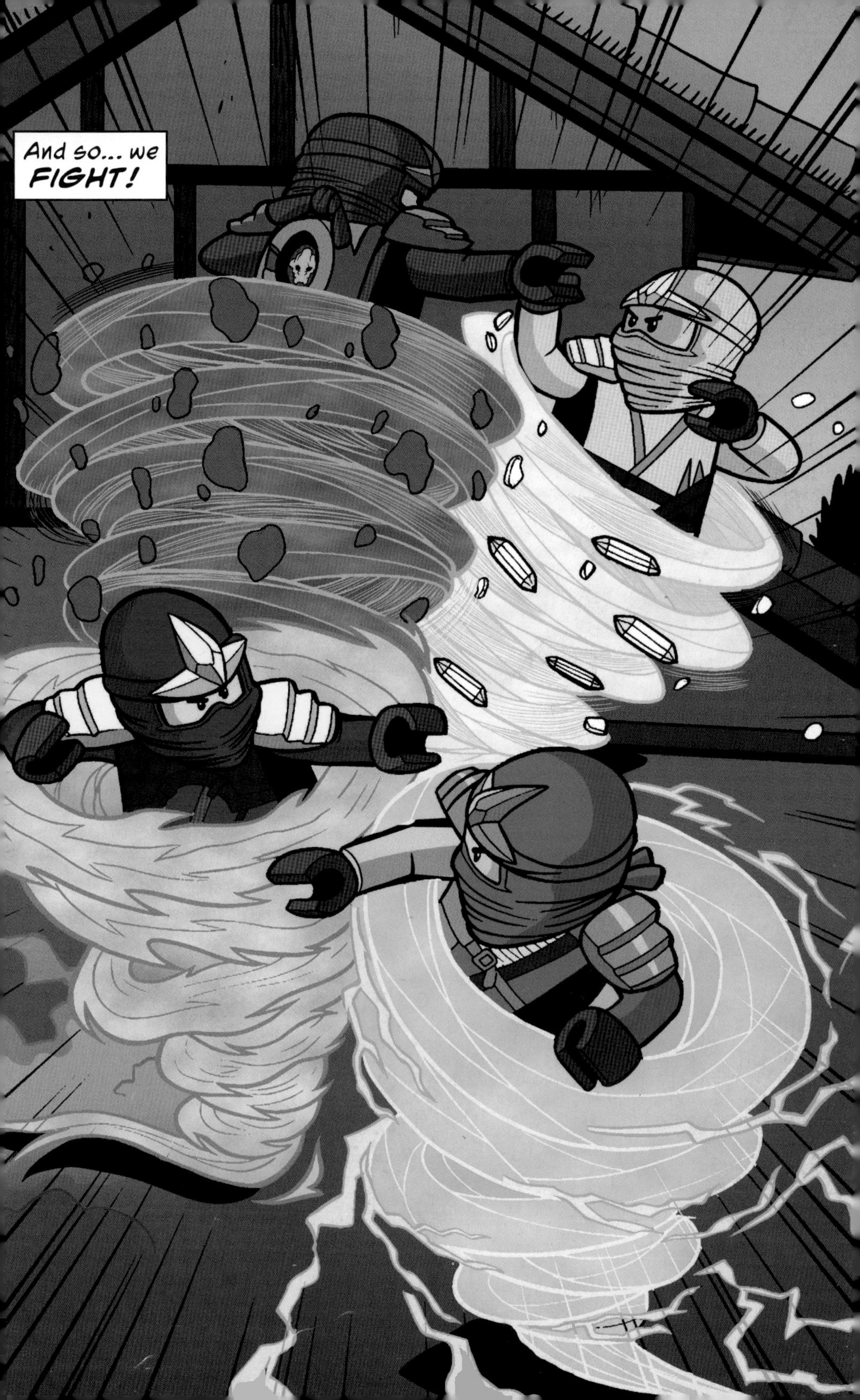
And so... we FIGHT!

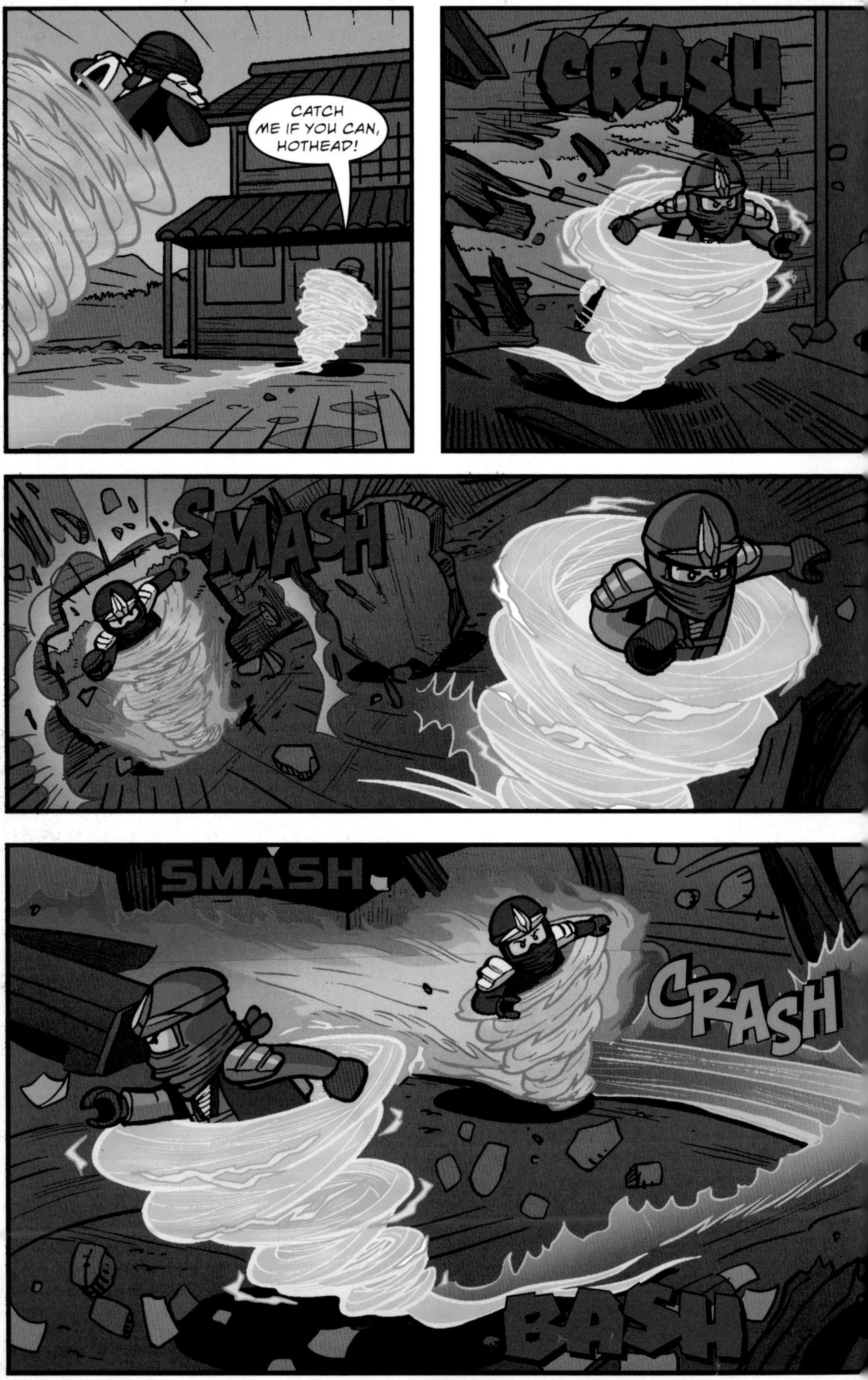
CATCH ME IF YOU CAN, HOTHEAD!
CRASH
SMASH
SMASH
CRASH
BASH

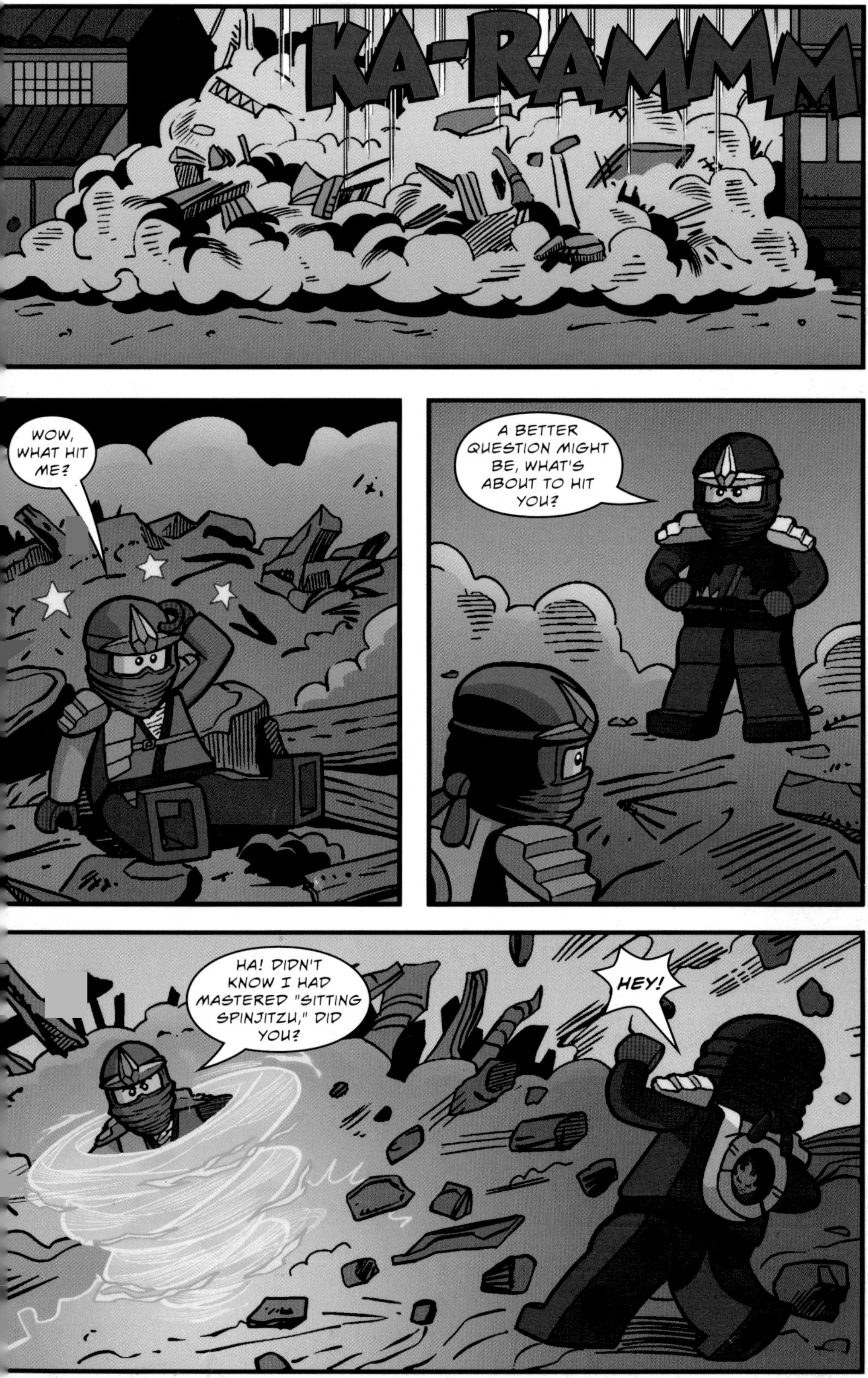
KA-RAMMM
WOW, WHAT HIT ME?
A BETTER QUESTION MIGHT BE, WHAT'S ABOUT TO HIT YOU?
HA! DIDN'T KNOW I HAD MASTERED "SITTING SPINJITZU," DID YOU?
HEY!

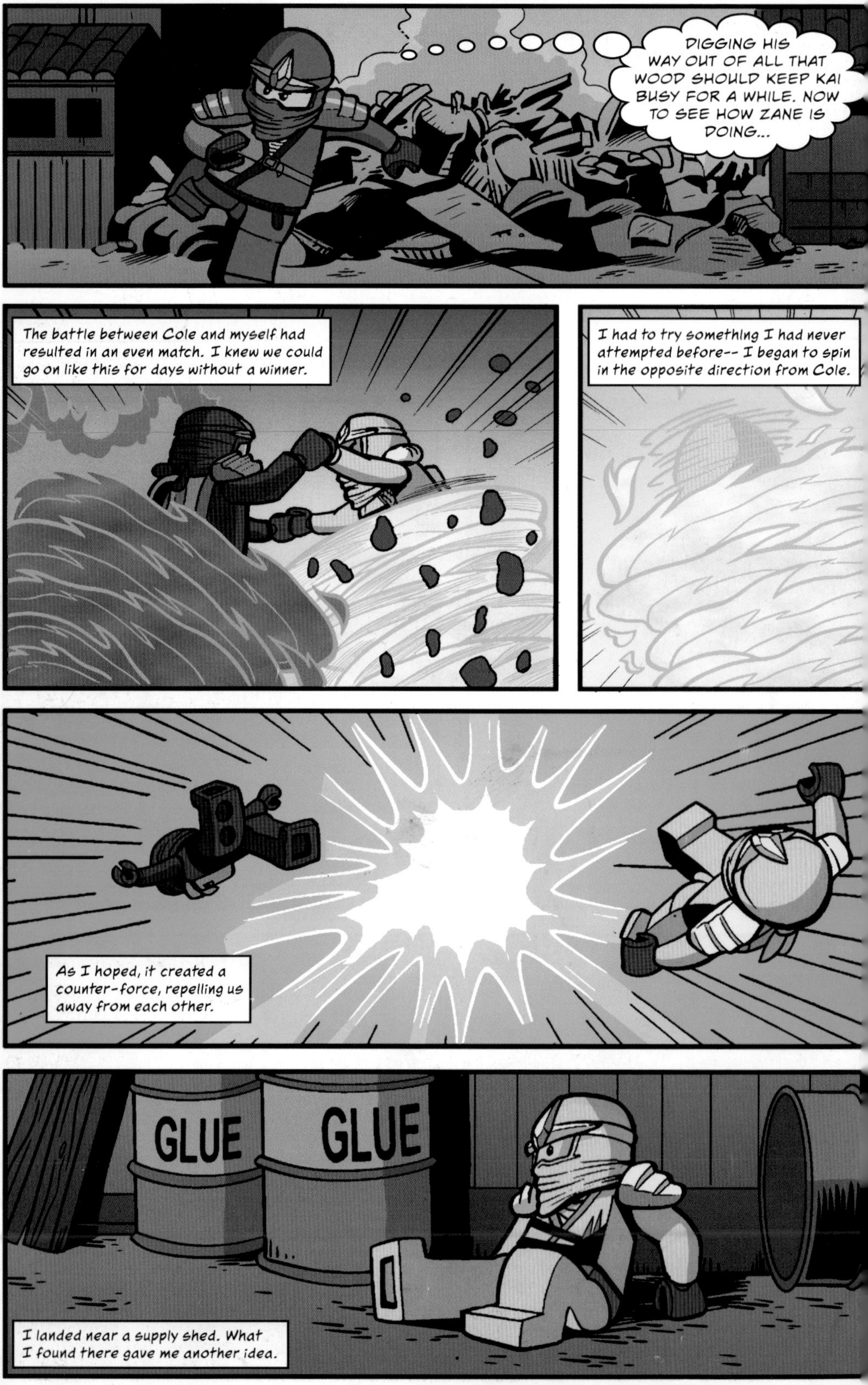
DIGGING HIS WAY OUT OF ALL THAT WOOD SHOULD KEEP KAI BUSY FOR A WHILE. NOW TO SEE HOW ZANE IS DOING...
The battle between Cole and myself had resulted in an even match. I knew we could go on like this for days without a winner.
I had to try something I had never attempted before-- I began to spin in the opposite direction from Cole.
As I hoped, it created a counter-force, repelling us away from each other.
GLUE
GLUE
I landed near a supply shed. What I found there gave me another idea.

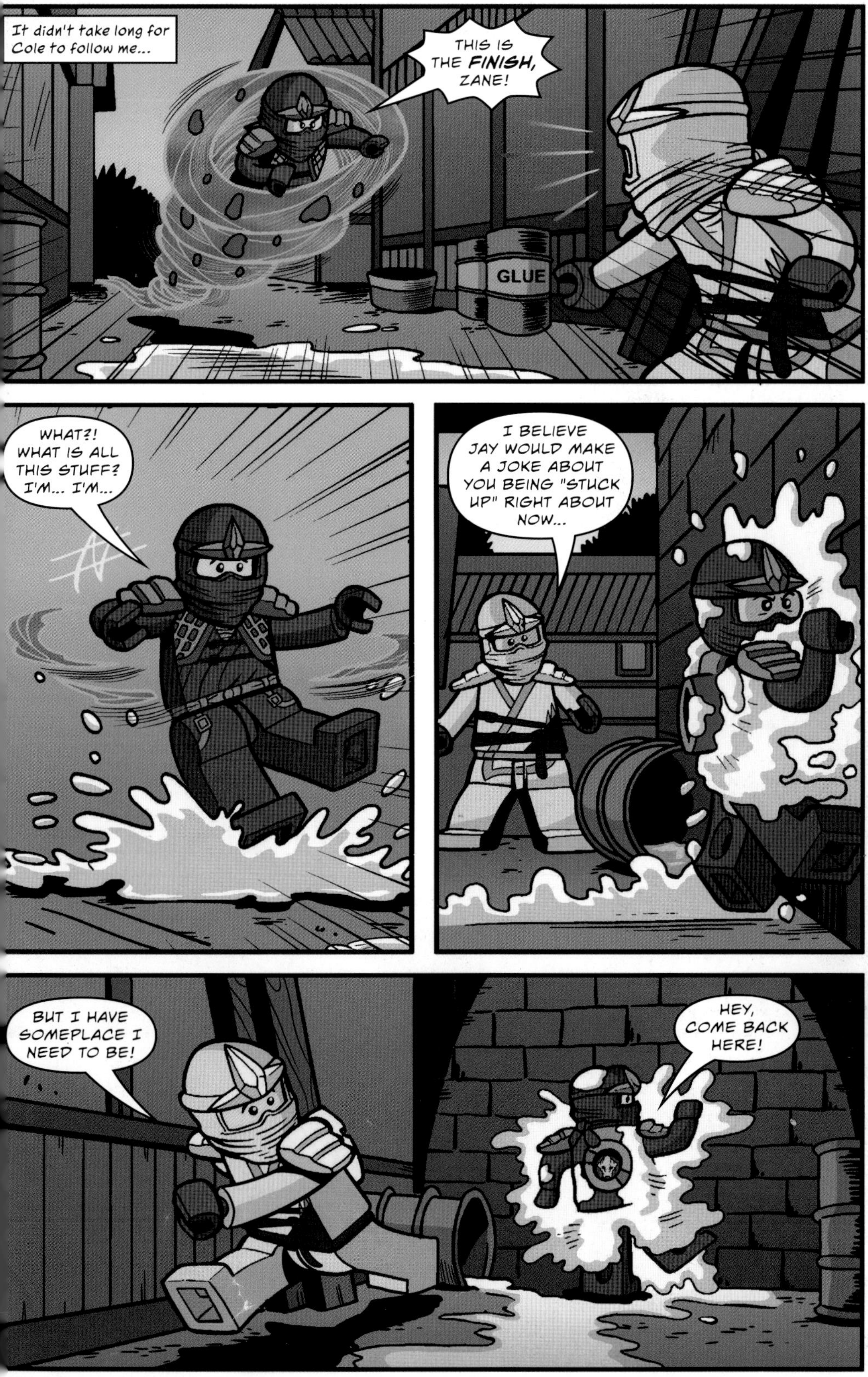
It didn't take long for Cole to follow me...
THIS IS THE FINISH, ZANE!
GLUE
WHAT?! WHAT IS ALL THIS STUFF? I'M... I'M...
I BELIEVE JAY WOULD MAKE A JOKE ABOUT YOU BEING "STUCK UP" RIGHT ABOUT NOW...
BUT I HAVE SOMEPLACE I NEED TO BE!
HEY, COME BACK HERE!

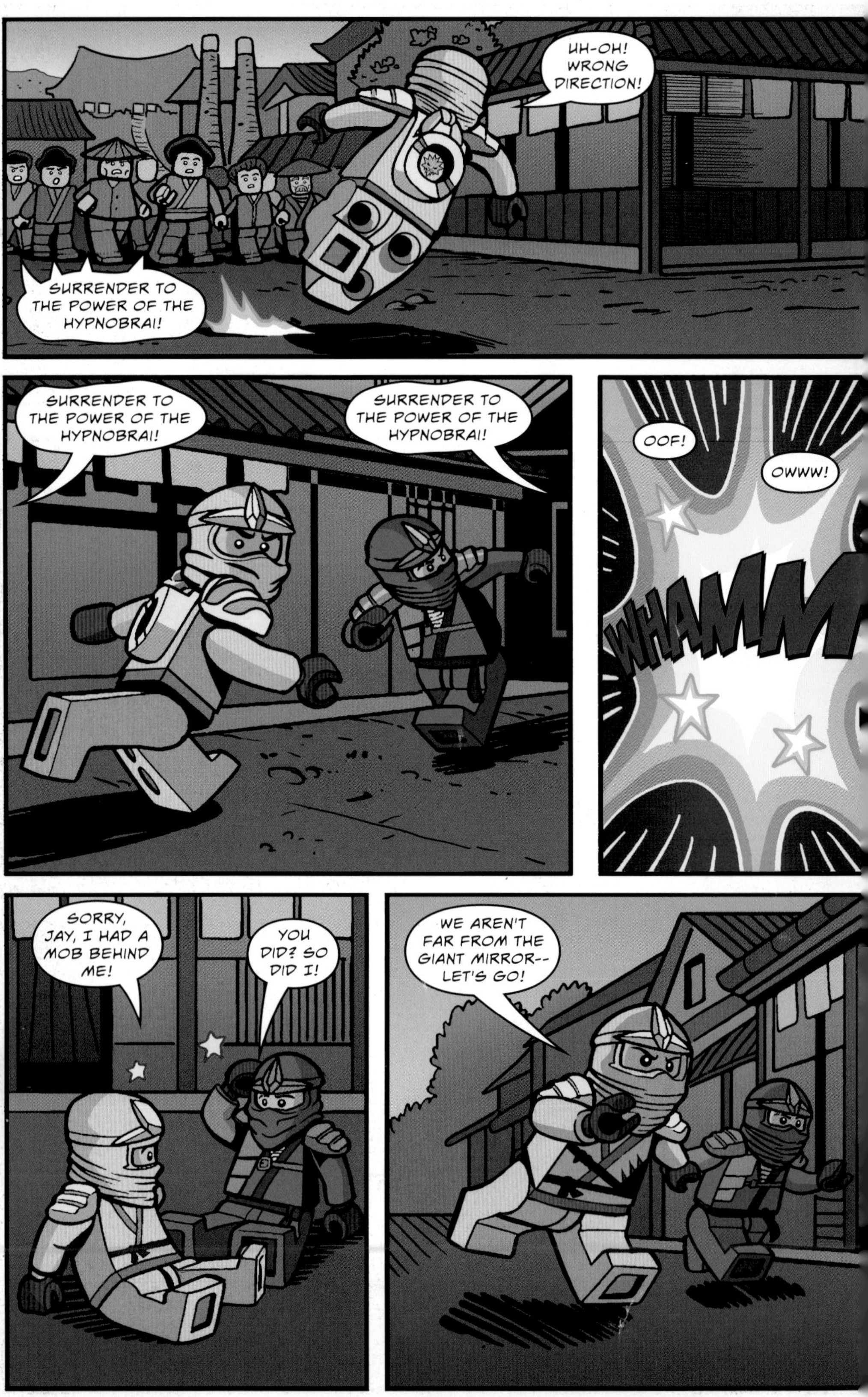
UH-OH! WRONG DIRECTION!
SURRENDER TO THE POWER OF THE HYPNOBRAI!
SURRENDER TO THE POWER OF THE HYPNOBRAI!
SURRENDER TO THE POWER OF THE HYPNOBRAI!
OOF!
OWWW!
WHAMM
SORRY, JAY, I HAD A MOB BEHIND ME!
YOU DID? SO DID I!
WE AREN'T FAR FROM THE GIANT MIRROR-- LET'S GO!

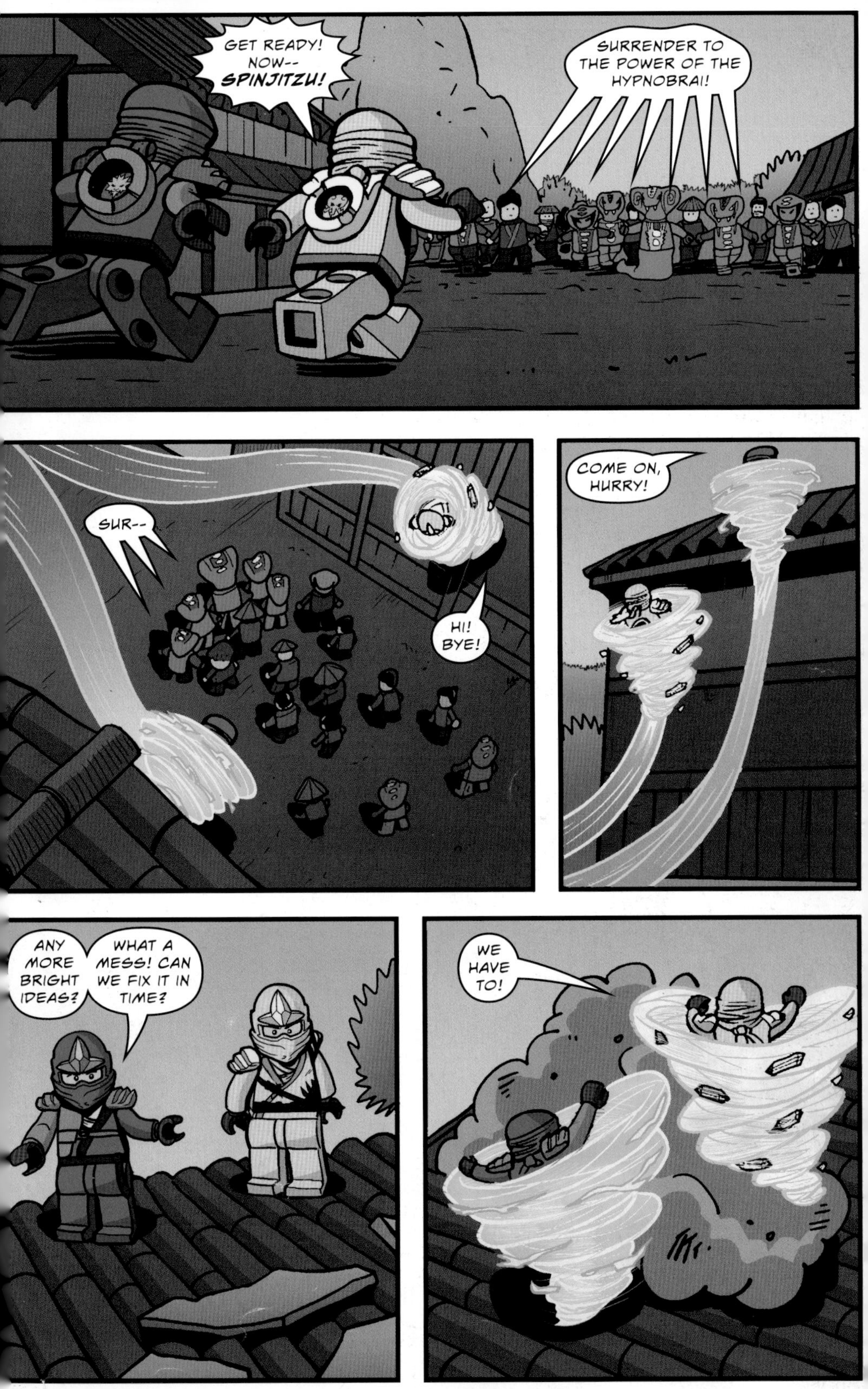
GET READY! NOW-- SPINJITZU!
SURRENDER TO THE POWER OF THE HYPNOBRAI!
SUR--
HI! BYE!
COME ON, HURRY!
ANY MORE BRIGHT IDEAS?
WHAT A MESS! CAN WE FIX IT IN TIME?
WE HAVE TO!

the SMURFS™

GRAPHIC NOVELS AVAILABLE AT BOOKSELLERS EVERYWHERE AND DIGITALLY FROM COMIXOLOGY.COM...

PURPLE SMURFS
PAPERCUTZ

Graphic Novel #1

THE SMURFS AND THE MAGIC FLUTE
PAPERCUTZ

Graphic Novel #2

THE SMURF KING
PAPERCUTZ

Graphic Novel #3

THE SMURFETTE
PAPERCUTZ

Graphic Novel #4

THE SMURFS AND THE EGG
PAPERCUTZ

Graphic Novel #5

THE SMURFS AND THE HOWLIBIRD
PAPERCUTZ

Graphic Novel #6

THE ASTRO SMURF
PAPERCUTZ

Graphic Novel #7

THE SMURF APPRENTICE
PAPERCUTZ

Graphic Novel #8

GARGAMEL AND THE SMURFS
PAPERCUTZ

Graphic Novel #9

THE RETURN OF THE SMURFETTE
PAPERCUTZ

Graphic Novel #10

THE SMURF OLYMPICS
PAPERCUTZ

Graphic Novel #11

SMURF VS. SMURF
PAPERCUTZ

Graphic Novel #12

EACH GRAPHIC NOVEL IS 100% SMURFY!

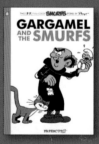